Tales from the Arabian Nights

James Riordan

Illustrated by Victor G Ambrus

Hamlyn
London · New York · Sydney · Toronto

For Catherine Gulnara

Sources

Sir Richard Burton, *The Arabian Nights' Entertainments*, London, 1954
Edward William Lane, *The Thousand and One Nights*, London, 1883
Andrew Lang, *Arabian Nights*, London, 1898
The Arabian Nights' Entertainments, London, 1899

Published 1983 by
The Hamlyn Publishing Group Limited
London · New York · Sydney · Toronto
Astronaut House, Feltham, Middlesex, England

ISBN 0 600 36693 6

Printed and bound by Graficromo s.a., Cordoba, Spain

Contents

Shaharazad

*In the name of Allah,
the compassionate, the
all-merciful, who raised
the heavens without pillars
and spread the earth out
like a bed.*

THE LIVES OF PEOPLE OF THE PAST should be a lesson to us all. We may read of the wonderful adventures of others; and they teach us modesty. We may learn of how other people live; and this teaches us understanding. Such are the tales of the Arabian nights or, as they are also known, tales of a thousand and one nights, with their exciting stories and their moral fables.

How did these stories come about?

It is related that there was in ancient times a Prince of Tartary who ruled the world from India to China, and he had two sons. When the great Prince died, he left his empire to the elder son, Shah Riyar; and the younger, Shah Zeman, became ruler of Samarkand. Each brother had ruled with justice for twenty years when Shah Zeman resolved to visit his brother and see how he was faring.

So he got ready for the journey, prepared tents and camels and mules, many servants and guards, and costly presents for his brother. Leaving his Vizier as governor, he set off on his long trip. However, he had not gone far when he suddenly recalled a gift for his brother that he had left behind.

On going back alone into his palace, he was shocked to find his wife asleep in bed with a slave by her side. A dark cloud of anger blurred his eyes and, drawing his sword, he cut off both their heads. Without more ado he hastened on his way.

When, after many months, he came to his brother's palace, the Shah of Tartary was overjoyed to see him. A holiday was proclaimed and the city was garlanded with flowers. But Shah Zeman, still shocked by the conduct of his wife, became pale and thin, and was morose. He was too ashamed to tell his brother of the cause, and when his brother went off to the hunt, Shah Zeman stayed behind.

Now, while Shah Riyar was at the chase, Shah Zeman gazed sadly from the palace windows into the courtyard beyond. All of a sudden, he was surprised to see his brother's unveiled wife come running out to sport and play with her male and female slaves. The revels continued until the close of day.

When Shah Zeman beheld this spectacle he told himself, 'Why, my brother's wife is even more sinful than my own.'

And the thought that his brother was even worse deceived cheered him up, and he began to eat and drink again.

When Shah Riyar returned from hunting he saw at once that the colour had come back to his brother's face and that his appetite was normal once again. On asking the reason for the change, his brother told the story of the two wives and their deceit. Shah Riyar was aghast: it surely could not be true about his wife! So it was arranged for him to pretend to go hunting once again, but secretly to stay at home, watching from his window.

As he looked down into the courtyard, he was shocked to see his wife enter with her slaves and do all his brother had described. The sport and dancing continued until afternoon prayer.

So upset were the brothers at the treachery of their wives and the shame of what went on behind their backs that they decided to renounce palace life and wander through the land. Slipping unnoticed from the palace, they therefore went into the world and journeyed about the empire for several days and nights. Finally, they arrived at the shore of a sea, and sat down to rest beside a tree. As night drew on, the sea suddenly began to seethe as up through the watery depths there came a pillar of black smoke. Struck with fear, the two brothers quickly climbed up the leafy tree and hid in its branches.

As they watched, they saw the pillar change its form into the most enormous genie, bearing a wooden chest upon his head. Seating himself beneath the tree, he opened the chest and there came forth a woman of human stature, as fair and beautiful as the sun. In booming voice, the genie said, 'O mistress mine, I desire to sleep a little. Watch over me while I slumber.'

With that, he placed his head upon her lap and closed his eyes, soon falling into a deep sleep.

Suddenly, hearing a noise above her in the tree, the damsel glanced up and noticed the brothers hiding there. At once she pushed the giant's head from her knees and called out, 'Come down, fear not the genie, I wish to embrace you handsome men.'

The brothers were reluctant, even afraid of the bold young woman. But she threatened them: 'If you do not descend, I shall rouse the genie and make him slay you right away.'

So, fearing the genie even more than the woman, they climbed down the tree; straightaway she embraced and kissed them both passionately. Then she took from her purse a string of rings: ninety eight, she said there were.

'They belonged to the men I have kissed without my master

9

knowing,' she said. 'Now give me yours to make up a hundred.'

They gave her the rings from their fingers, and she laughed in their faces, saying, 'Never trust a woman, nor rely upon her promise; for her faithfulness depends upon her passion. She will give you false affection, yet deceive you as she will.'

When the two Shahs heard these words, they felt pity for the poor genie, who was even worse deceived than themselves. And they both returned, each to his own realm.

The first thing Shah Riyar did on his return was have his wife and all his slaves beheaded; then he made a vow: each time he took a new wife she would die before the night was out. That way he could never be deceived again.

Thus it continued for three terrible years until hardly any young women were left alive. The Shah would send his Vizier to find him a victim; and the Vizier had been warned that if he did not succeed he would pay for it with his head. One day, the poor Vizier looked everywhere for another maiden without success, and at last went home to bid a sorrowful farewell to his family.

Now the Vizier had two daughters: Dunyazad and Shaharazad. Both were young and beautiful and so far the Vizier, who loved them dearly, had kept them hidden from the Shah. The elder girl, Shaharazad, had collected a thousand books of stories about the past; she knew the works of poets, the tales of merchants and mariners, and the histories of kings and queens. When she heard of her father's threatened fate, she at once implored him to let her wed the Shah.

In tears, her poor father begged her to change her mind; he would rather die himself. But she was adamant. What is more, she had a plan

And so began the first of the tales.

to save them all.

'When I am with the Shah,' she told her sister, 'I shall send for you as my last wish; and you will ask me to relate one last story before I die. If Allah wills it, my story shall lead to our salvation.'

Her father then led her to the Shah who, when he saw her, was determined she would die by sunrise. She was so beautiful that he thought she must be very deceitful. As night drew on and the time came near for her execution, she asked the Shah for one last favour. 'I wish to see my sister before I die,' she said.

'So be it,' replied the Shah.

Shortly after, Dunyazad arrived and begged her sister, as planned, 'Dear Sister, do tell me one of your marvellous stories to pass the waking hour.'

'If the Shah permits it,' said Shaharazad, 'I shall be pleased to relate a story about a young boy and a lamp.'

The Shah, who enjoyed listening to stories, nodded his assent. And so began the first of the tales, the first of the Arabian nights. Shaharazad told the tales so that she broke off at an exciting part with the rising of the sun. For it was then the Shah intended to have her put to death. But so eager was he to hear the end of the story that he spared her for one more night.

Of course, in the end, after a thousand and one nights, the Shah renounced his evil vow, regretting his former wickedness and lack of trust in women. From then on, Queen Shaharazad and Shah Riyar lived together in peace and happiness, and her stories were recorded for all the world to read.

This book contains some of her favourite tales.

Aladdin and his Wonderful Lamp

T IS SAID THAT IN A CERTAIN CITY in China there once lived a poor tailor who had a son named Aladdin. Now this son was an idle, good-for-nothing boy who played in the streets all day and never obeyed his parents. Aladdin's father died when the boy was fifteen, and the poor mother was left to bring him up.

One day, as Aladdin was playing in the street as usual, a stranger came up to him and said, 'Greetings, bold and clever youth. You are surely the son of an honourable father. May I ask his name?'

'My father is dead,' Aladdin replied. 'He was Mustafa the tailor.'

At that, the stranger (who, you should know, was really a wicked wizard) embraced the boy, crying, 'I thought as much; I saw the likeness. I am your father's brother! Here, take these two gold coins and lead me to your mother.'

Aladdin willingly showed the rich stranger to where he lived and at once gave his mother the two gold coins. No sooner did the man enter the house than he fell to his knees, weeping for his brother's memory. Several times he kissed the sofa on which his brother used to sit, crying out in grief, 'My poor brother! How miserable I am not to return in time to see you.'

Aladdin's mother was much surprised, since her late husband had never mentioned any brother. But the stranger calmed her suspicions, saying he had been forty years out of his native land, journeying to India, Arabia, Syria and Egypt, finally settling in Africa; and there he had made his fortune. This was his first trip home.

The evening passed. Aladdin's mother prepared a fine supper, using the stranger's two gold coins to buy food and drink, and it was late when the man returned to the inn where he was staying the night. The next day he returned to entertain Aladdin and his mother with stories of his adventures in other lands. The boy was much taken with his uncle and his wonderful tales. On the third day, the stranger invited Aladdin to accompany him 'to see something strange and exciting', as he said.

The wizard led Aladdin out of the city, on and on until they reached a wooded valley between two high hills. He recounted amazing stories

No sooner did the man enter the
house than he fell to his knees,
weeping for his brother's memory.

all along the way to distract the boy from the journey – for, truth to tell, Aladdin was growing frightened because they were so far from home.

'We will halt here,' the wizard said, as they came to a clump of trees. 'Go and fetch some sticks to build a fire.'

When Aladdin had gathered up a bundle of dry sticks and brushwood, his uncle cast some magic powder on the tinder and right away flames sprang up higher than the trees. Mumbling more magic words, the wizard moved his hands across the flames and they instantly fizzled out, leaving a charred black patch upon the ground.

As Aladdin watched in astonishment, the black earth parted to reveal a slab of stone with a brass ring embedded in it.

By now Aladdin was trembling with fright. And his uncle's voice had changed: he was no longer kind and polite, but cruel and commanding.

'Now listen, stupid boy,' the man snarled; 'under this stone there is a treasure which only you can fetch: so it is ordained. Otherwise I would have taken it myself and not bothered with the likes of you. Take hold of the ring and pull up the stone.'

Aladdin did as he was told and raised the stone with ease, uncovering a flight of steps.

'Go down the steps,' the wizard said, 'and you will find three great halls; in each one you will see four urns filled with gold, silver or jewels. Do not touch them. If you do, you will die at once and your bones will rot there forever. The third hall leads into an orchard, at the end of which there stands a wall; and in that wall there is a niche holding a lighted lamp. Pour out its oil and bring me the lamp.'

Thereupon the wizard took a ring from his finger and handed it to the trembling boy.

'Take this ring,' he said. 'It will protect you against evil, as long as you do what I have instructed.'

Aladdin stepped carefully down the steps, one by one. It was not dark at all: his way seemed to be lit by dozens of concealed candles. As he reached the bottom of the steps he found himself in a tall cavern with two giant urns on either side: they were brimful of glittering gold and silver coins. He was sorely tempted to touch the coins, just to see if they were real; but mindful of the wizard's words, he passed on by.

Next, he squeezed through an opening and emerged into an even bigger cave, this one furnished with four great urns filled with diamonds and pearls; there were so many they had tumbled out upon the earthen floor. How he longed to touch them. But he dared not and passed on by.

Entering a third tall cave, he saw four more urns, this time spilling out rubies and amber upon the path. He set aside temptation yet again and passed on through some iron gates into an orchard, where it was as light as day. Birds were singing, the fig and date trees were in full fruit

and beautiful flowers gave the air a delicate fragrance. But, mindful of the wizard's instructions, he made his way through the trees until he reached the stone wall which the wizard had described to him.

And there in the centre, within a niche, glowed a lamp – just an ordinary, dusty, dull pewter lamp of the kind that could be bought cheaply at any bazaar. He took it down, poured out the oil and tucked it inside his coat. Then he made his way back through the halls until he reached the flight of steps. Just as he began to climb up, he heard the wizard give a cruel laugh and mutter to himself, 'Ah-ha, now the lamp is mine and I can kill that foolish boy.'

But he spoke too soon, not thinking that Aladdin could hear him. The boy quickly realized that the lamp was his only chance of survival, and he refused to give it up.

'Since you are going to kill me, you shall not have the lamp,' the boy shouted up the steps.

The wizard flew into a dreadful rage and, in his anger, slammed down the slab of stone, stamped his foot and flew himself back to Africa.

In truth, the wizard had heard about the magic lamp on his travels; he had been told it could only be his from another's hands. And he had chosen Aladdin because he looked just the sort of foolish, idle fellow to do the job. Now, furious at being disobeyed, he gave up his quest and left the boy to die.

Poor Aladdin, meanwhile, sat upon the steps yelling for help and bewailing his destiny. He shouted until he was hoarse; but it was no good. No one would ever hear him in that lonely valley. Finally, wringing his hands in despair, he chanced to rub the wizard's ring. Until then he had not given it a thought.

All at once, an enormous genie appeared, so tall there was hardly space for him to stand in the cave. 'I am the genie of the ring,' he boomed. 'To hear is to obey, O master. What is your command?'

At first Aladdin was too scared to speak. But since his life depended on it, he stammered out the words, 'Take me home.'

No sooner had he spoken than he found himself borne through the air and set down in his mother's house. The poor woman was as startled as her son at his sudden return. But when he told her all about his adventures and the false uncle, she was glad to be rid of the man and to have Aladdin safely home. Tired out from his journey, Aladdin went straight to bed and slept soundly late into the following day.

Next morning his mother was up as usual at dawn, anxious to cook her son a hearty meal. Unfortunately, there was nothing in the house and no money to buy bread or eggs. Seeing the dull old lamp upon the table, Aladdin's mother had an idea: she would clean it up and take it to market to sell. That way she would have a few coins for food.

So, taking a rag, she began to rub the lamp . . .

Imagine her surprise when there came a great clap of thunder and a cloud of smoke, and a huge genie appeared before her, booming out, 'To hear is to obey, O mistress. I am the genie of the lamp. What is your command?'

That was too much for the poor woman: she fell to the floor in a faint. But the noise had woken up her son, who knew how to deal with genies by this time, and called out from his bed, 'Bring us food and drink.'

In no time at all the genie had brought a large silver tray bearing twelve golden dishes of the most delicious meats, six iced cakes and two flasks of sherbet. Placing them gently on the floor, he bowed and vanished in a puff of smoke – before Aladdin's mother could recover from her swoon.

Mother and son now proceeded to eat the best meal they had ever tasted. But at the end of it Aladdin's mother grumbled to her son, 'Now get rid of that awful lamp; I think I would die if that ugly genie showed his face again. And while you are at it, sell that ring you mentioned, too. We don't want genies in this house. What would the neighbours say?'

However, being disobedient, Aladdin did not sell the lamp or ring. Instead, he dug a hole beneath the floor and concealed them both there. From then on he and his mother lived well enough on the money they made from selling the silver tray and the twelve golden dishes.

Five years passed by, and Aladdin changed from a foolish, idle boy to an intelligent, handsome young man.

One day, as the Emperor's lovely daughter was being carried through the streets in her sedan, Aladdin chanced to catch a glimpse of her. That was enough, for the young man fell deeply in love at first sight. Later that day he told his mother of his feelings for Princess Buddir.

'I love her more than I can tell,' he said. 'My mind is made up: I am going to ask the Emperor for his daughter's hand in marriage.'

His poor mother was aghast. 'You must be mad,' she cried. 'How can a commoner like you take a royal wife?'

So Aladdin told his mother of his plan. He had not disposed of the wonderful lamp after all, so he would dig it up, summon the genie of the lamp and use him to help win the Princess's love. Thereupon Aladdin called up the genie.

'To hear is to obey, O master,' the huge genie boomed. 'What is your command?'

'Bring me a pile of precious gems,' Aladdin boldly said.

In a flash there lay on the table an enormous dish of sparkling diamonds, blood red rubies, huge pearls and opals, emeralds and jade. The gleaming jewels so dazzled Aladdin and his mother that their eyes smarted from the sight.

'Now, Mother, please take this dish of gems to the Emperor and tell him of my love for his daughter.'

Obediently, his mother covered the tray in a large white napkin and carried it to the palace. She was let in by the guards, once she had shown her tray, and was given an audience before the Emperor. Placing the dish in front of him, she sank to her knees, kowtowing to the monarch, bowing low so that her head touched the floor. After mumbling her humble greetings, she uncovered her tray of sparkling gems.

Everyone at the Emperor's court let out a gasp as the jewels flooded the chamber with brilliant light.

Aladdin's mother explained her mission, keeping her head pressed to the floor and not daring to gaze upon the monarch. However, though eager to own the jewels, the Emperor was not so happy at the woman's proposition. But such was his greed that he pretended to agree.

'Come back in three months' time,' he said, 'and then the wedding will be arranged.'

When this news was conveyed to Aladdin he thought himself the happiest man in the world. He counted every hour of every week until the joyful day arrived. He then sent his mother back to the palace, where she reminded the Emperor of his pledge. Seeing the ragged woman before him, the mighty king was less keen than ever to surrender his daughter. But all the court had been witness to his promise of three months before, so he could not go back on his word. After a

*Placing the dish in front of him,
she bowed low so that her
head touched the floor.*

hasty consultation with his Vizier, the Emperor turned to Aladdin's mother and said, 'Certainly I shall keep my word: your son may wed the Princess Buddir, but on one condition: first he must send me forty golden dishes of precious gems borne by forty slaves. And these must be preceded by forty richly-dressed servants carrying jewels.'

'He'll be a long time managing that,' whispered the Emperor to his Vizier with a wink.

'It won't take long, Mother,' said Aladdin when he heard the news. 'I'll send the treasure right away.'

And summoning up the genie of the lamp, Aladdin told him of the royal command. In a flash a long train of forty slaves and forty servants, all richly dressed and each bearing, in turn, a golden dish of pearls, diamonds, rubies and emeralds, was marching solemnly to court. As the grand procession passed through the streets, Aladdin's mother at

its head (richly dressed in robes provided by the genie), Aladdin sat expectantly at home, waiting to be summoned.

The crowds that thronged the route had never seen so grand a sight; they cheered and cheered as the long line of slaves and servants passed through the palace portals and entered the Emperor's court, slaves to the left, servants to the right. And as they came before the Emperor's throne, they each knelt down, touching the carpet with their heads and placing their trays before the throne. When the last had made his bow, they all stood up, arms crossed over their chests.

When all the court was silent, Aladdin's mother advanced to the throne, bowed down and said, 'Sire, my son presents his compliments, begs you to accept his humble gift and keep your promise.'

The Emperor hesitated no more. 'Go and tell your son to come at once,' he said. 'The wedding will be held this very day.'

The crowds had never seen so grand a sight.

21

But Aladdin was in no hurry.

First he rubbed the lamp and, as the genie appeared in a flash of light and puff of smoke, he gave an order: 'Wash and scrub me in a bath until I'm shining clean; then dress me in robes which befit a prince.'

Straightaway Aladdin found himself naked in a marble bath, with the genie's great hands washing, scrubbing and, finally, rubbing him with all manner of oils and perfumes. Then he was dressed in robes of silk embroidered with gold, set upon a magnificent white horse and, at the head of forty dusky slaves bearing purses of ten thousand golden pieces, he rode sedately to the palace.

As the splendid procession wound through the streets, Aladdin threw handfuls of gold pieces to the crowd lining the route. Just before the palace, he summoned the genie of the lamp once more, saying, 'Slave of the lamp, build me a palace of white marble set with jasper, agate, lapis lazuli and other precious stones; let its inside walls be alternately of gold and silver bricks. And let there be spacious courtyards with crystal fountains, verdant gardens and stables for a thousand white Arabian steeds. And, of course, a treasure house filled to

the roof with silver and gold.'

The palace was built to his specification before he could blink an eye.
How amazed the Emperor of China was to behold a red carpet running
from his own palace gates to this glittering new residence next door.

'It must be Aladdin's palace,' he said to his Vizier. 'I will despatch my
daughter there forthwith.'

Thus, the Princess Buddir went, attended by her maidservants, to the
new palace where she was met by Aladdin at the gates. How charmed
she was by all about her and, of course, she fell in love at once with the
handsome, rich, enchanting young man.

And so they lived in peace and contentment.

As the years passed by, Aladdin gained the love and blessings of the
people for his generosity and his modest ways; thus, when a man or
woman made a promise, they often did so 'By Aladdin's Head', as they
would say.

And there my story would have ended had not ill fortune chanced to
intervene. For one day that wicked wizard heard on the wind of gossip
about the splendid palace and its occupant Prince Aladdin. He recognized the name at once.

'It must be that stupid boy,' he snarled with rage, setting off at once
to seek him out.

First he had to retrieve the magic lamp. So, when Aladdin was not at
home, the wizard stood outside the palace with a basketful of shiny,
new, copper lamps, calling 'New lamps for old! New lamps for old!'

A crowd soon gathered, laughing at the fool who would exchange a
new lamp for an old one. This hubbub reached Princess Buddir's ears.
And when she learned of the old man's offer she thought she would
please her husband by exchanging his dirty old lamp, which she had
seen on a shelf in his room, for a shining new one. She sent out a slave to
do the deal.

As soon as he had the magic lamp safely in his grasp, the wicked
wizard quickly made his way to a lonely spot where he eagerly rubbed
the lamp. With a flash and a puff of smoke, the genie of the lamp
appeared, booming out, 'To hear is to obey, O master. What is your
command?'

'I command you,' said the wizard, 'to take me and Aladdin's palace
to Africa.'

Quicker than it takes to say these words the deed was done.

Later that day, as Aladdin was riding home, he was seized by the
Emperor's guards and dragged unceremoniously before him.

'Where is my daughter?' shouted the Emperor in a rage.

'Why, she is where I left her,' replied Aladdin, surprised.

'Then look out of my window and tell me what you see,' the
monarch yelled.

Aladdin did as he was bid and gasped in alarm, for there was nothing

23

to be seen but empty space. When he had recovered from the shock, he begged for time to solve the mystery.

'To be sure, the palace has vanished,' he said, 'but it is not my doing. Grant me, I beg you, forty days' grace, and if I have not found your daughter by then, you may strike off my head yourself.'

'So be it,' replied the Emperor gravely.

For several days, Aladdin wandered about the city, asking everyone he met whether they had seen the palace or his wife. But he had no success. At last he came to a river outside the city; throwing himself down upon its bank, he sobbed out his heart for his lost wife. Yet as he dried his eyes, he accidentally rubbed the magic ring upon his finger and summoned up the genie of the ring.

'Genie,' Aladdin cried hopefully, 'bring back my palace and my wife.'

'That, O master, is not within my power,' said the genie solemnly. 'I am the slave of the ring, not the lamp.'

'Then take me to my wife at least,' Aladdin begged.

Hardly had he spoken than he was carried to Africa and set down beneath his wife's palace window. At dawn next day, the Princess chanced to look out and see her husband sleeping there. At once she sent down her maid to bring up her dear, beloved Aladdin. After embracing and shedding tears, the Princess told Aladdin how she had exchanged his old lamp for a new one.

'Where is the old lamp now?' Aladdin asked.

'The wizard keeps it with him all the time,' she said. 'For he told me so and showed me where it was hidden inside his robe.'

24

Together they hatched a plan, then Aladdin just had time to hide before the wizard entered, shouting out, 'Your husband is dead, his head struck off by your father's hand. So now you are mine.'

The Princess pretended to be resigned to her fate and, to show her acceptance, she poured out two goblets of wine. But, unobserved, she sprinkled a sleeping draught into one; and this goblet she handed to the wizard.

Delighted at the success of his scheme, the wizard took the goblet and drained it to the dregs.

As he fell back in a deep sleep upon the couch, Aladdin emerged from behind the curtains and, bending over the wizard, took the lamp from inside his robe.

Then, taking his sharp dagger, he cut out the villain's heart.

'Now,' Aladdin said to his wife, 'you will witness the magic of this lamp.'

With that he rubbed the lamp and, with a flash and a puff of smoke, the genie suddenly appeared.

'To hear is to obey, O master,' he said.

'I command you to return this palace to its former home,' said Aladdin firmly.

Immediately the palace was taken swiftly through the air from Africa to China; and the journey took only half the blink of an eye.

The Emperor was overjoyed to have his daughter back and to see the shining palace alongside his own again. Thereafter, Aladdin and his wife, the Princess Buddir, lived in peace and, when at last the Emperor died, they reigned together for many long and happy years.

Aladdin took the lamp from inside the wizard's robe.

The Fisherman and the Brass Bottle

THERE WAS ONCE AN OLD FISHERMAN who was so poor he barely had enough to support his wife and children. Every day at noon he went to fish down by the shore, hoping to net something for his family to eat.

One day, when he had cast his nets into the sea, he went to pull them up and found them very heavy. Thinking he had caught an enormous fish, he pulled and pulled until the nets lay on the shore. To his dismay all he found at the bottom of them was a big brass bottle with a leaden stopper in its mouth. Still, at least he could sell the bottle at the market for a piece of gold or two; but as he moved the jar he felt something heavy roll about inside.

'I must open it up and see what it holds,' he muttered to himself excitedly.

So, taking a knife, he prised out the stopper, laid the jar on its side and shook it hard so that its contents could spill out. To his surprise, thick smoke came from the jar, spiralling right up to the sky and forming a thick mist over sea and shore.

As he gazed astounded at the smoke, he saw it form into a lofty pillar; and a genie gradually took shape, with his feet upon the shore and his head piercing the clouds. What a frightening sight! His head was like the dome of the biggest mosque; his hands were like giant rakes; his legs were like the masts of the tallest sailing ship; his mouth was like a black cavern with giant boulders blocking the entrance; his nostrils were like great trumpets, his eyes like flashing lamps.

When the fisherman beheld the genie, his legs turned to jelly, his teeth chattered together and his mouth went as dry as the desert sands. And when the genie spoke, which sounded just like the seven winds roaring together, the fisherman had to stop up his ears with his hands.

'Know this,' the genie boomed, 'for my evil ways I was cast by Suleiman the prophet into the ocean depths. I have been imprisoned in that bottle for these last six hundred years. At first I thought I would reward the man who set me free; but as the years rolled by, my ire rose and I vowed to kill the first man I set my eyes on. So prepare to die!'

With a sandstorm swirling about him from the genie's breath, the poor fisherman trembled with fear and desperately sought a way to save himself.

'Since I must die,' he said, 'pray tell me one thing first. How did a giant as tall as you squeeze into such a tiny bottle? I do not believe you were in there at all.'

The genie roared even more loudly that the man should doubt his powers.

'I can turn myself into any shape I want!' he shouted at the fisherman.

'I cannot believe you until I see you in the jar again,' replied the fisherman.

At that, the genie swiftly dissolved into smoke and poured himself with a rush back into the bottle until no smoke remained. Straightaway, the fisherman snatched up the leaden stopper and sealed the mouth of the jar, crying out in triumph, 'Now, genie, I did nothing bad to you, yet you would kill me. So you can go back into the sea and stay there till judgement day.'

Thereupon the fisherman took the brass bottle to the sea and went to throw it in. Meanwhile, the genie hollered and yelled from inside the bottle.

'Fisherman,' he begged, 'for the love of Allah the all-merciful, let me out. If you set me free I will make you rich beyond your dreams.'

So it went on, the genie pleading and promising, the fisherman firm and unyielding. Finally, when he had made the genie swear by Allah, the fisherman gave in: he opened the jar once more and smoke poured forth, giving shape to the hideous genie.

The genie's first act on being freed was to kick the brass bottle into the sea – not a good omen for the fisherman, who began to think he was now doomed. But, plucking up his courage, he reminded the genie of his vow before Allah the all-seeing and all-merciful.

The genie laughed scornfully. 'Take up your nets and follow me,' he bellowed.

Striding quickly off he headed for the town and, with the fisherman running in pursuit, passed through it, went up a steep hill and down the other side into a long desert valley. In the centre lay a shimmering lake, surrounded by four hills. It was here the genie stopped, ordering the fisherman to cast his nets again. This he did and when he pulled them in he discovered he had caught four fish, each of a different hue: one white, one red, one blue and one a yellowish-brown.

'Take them to the Sultan,' said the genie. 'He will reward you generously. But hear me well: you may fish here again, but never more than once a day. And now I bid you farewell and commend you to Allah's care.'

So saying, he stamped hard upon the earth, which instantly opened up and swallowed him without a trace.

The fisherman meanwhile returned to the town, hardly able to believe his adventures. At the palace the Sultan was astonished when he saw the fish, for he had never seen the like.

'Take them to the cook and have them fried for supper,' he told his Grand Vizier.

As the Vizier took out the fish on a golden tray, the Sultan thanked the fisherman and gave him four hundred pieces of gold in reward. Happy and more than somewhat relieved, the fisherman returned home to his family; never would they want for food again.

In the meantime, at the palace, the cook had taken the fish, cleaned them, put them in a frying pan, and set them on a stove to cook. Scarcely had the fish begun to sizzle, however, than the kitchen wall parted like a curtain and in came a tall stately maid, richly dressed in a blue silk gown with costly rings upon her fingers and jewelled earrings. In her hand she carried a bamboo cane. Dipping it into the frying pan, she asked three times, 'Fish, O fish, are you faithful to your vow?'

At the third time of asking, the fish raised their heads out of the pan and answered, 'Yes, yes, we are. If you return, we return; if you come, we come; and if you forsake us, we duly do the same.'

Thereupon the stately maid overturned the pan, spilling the fish into the fire. Then she left the way she came, the wall closing up behind her.

Now, when she witnessed this, the poor cook fainted clean away; and when she recovered, the four fish were burned to a cinder. As the Vizier commanded her to bring in the Sultan's tea, she wept and told him what had happened. And he, good man, did not tell the Sultan, but sent for the fisherman instead, instructing him to fetch four more fish like those before.

Accordingly, the fisherman went to the lake, cast his nets and drew in four fish exactly as before: one white, one blue, one red and one yellowish-brown. He took them forthwith to the Vizier, who handed him one hundred golden pieces and said to the cook, 'Fry them in my presence, so that I may test your tale.'

The cook therefore prepared the fish and put them in the frying pan. Hardly had they begun to sizzle than the wall opened up just like a curtain and in came the stately damsel as before, carrying the bamboo cane. She dipped it into the pan and asked loudly, 'Fish, O fish, are you faithful to your vow?'

At the third time of asking, the fish raised their heads and answered as before, 'Yes, yes, we are. If you return, we return; if you come, we come; and if you forsake us, we duly do the same.'

Thereupon the damsel overturned the pan, spilling the fish into the fire, before returning whence she had come.

'This is an event we cannot hide from the Sultan,' said the Grand Vizier.

So he went to tell the Sultan about the fish.

'This is a marvel I must see for myself,' exclaimed the Sultan. 'Have the fisherman catch us four more fish.'

Again the fisherman went to the lake, caught four such fish and brought them to the palace, receiving his third reward: this time three hundred golden coins.

'Now,' said the Sultan to his cook, 'prepare the fish right here and now.'

Just as before, the wall opened up and the stately maid entered holding a bamboo cane. She ignored the assembled throng and addressed only the fish: 'Fish, O fish, are you faithful to your vow?'

Upon which, the fish raised their heads at the third time of asking and answered as before, 'Yes, yes, we are. If you return, we return; if you come, we come; and if you forsake us, we duly do the same.'

Thereupon the maiden overturned the pan with her cane and went off through the wall. In great astonishment, the Sultan sent for the fisherman and questioned him about the fish. And the man told the story: of the genie, of the brass bottle, of the lake between four hills.

When he had heard him out, the Sultan at once called his army together and, with the fisherman as guide, the long train of soldiers set off across the hill and down into the desert valley until they reached the shimmering lake. And when the Sultan gazed down into the waters of the lake, he saw them full of fish of the four hues: white, blue, red and yellowish-brown.

'Have any of you set eyes on this lake before?' he asked his men.
They all said no.

Then said the Sultan, 'By Allah, I shall not rest until I learn the story of this lake and its strange fish.'

Thereupon he ordered his troops to camp around the lake and summoned his Grand Vizier.

'I intend to go out alone this night,' he said, 'and see what lies beyond the four hills. Perhaps I'll find the key to unlock this mystery.'

Thus, as soon as it was dark, the Sultan strapped on his sword and set off alone across the valley, seeking an answer to the riddle of the lake. He journeyed through the night into the following day; and soon after dawn he spied, far in the distance, something black looming up into the sky. As he approached he saw it was a palace of black stone.

Coming up, he boldly entered by the open doors and passed through halls and chambers, calling out to left and right that he was a traveller seeking food and rest.

No one answered.

As last, he emerged into an inner courtyard which had a crystal fountain playing in the centre with water spouting from the mouths of four golden lions. Around the fountain flew a flock of doves, prevented from flying off by a rooftop net.

The Sultan sat down upon the fountain steps, wondering at the empty, silent palace. Yet as he sat musing on the meaning of it all he

As he approached he saw it was a palace of black stone.

thought he heard a soft, sad voice singing from beyond a curtain at the far end of the yard. Moving towards the wistful song, he pulled aside the curtain to reveal a handsome, richly-attired young man sitting upon a couch. At the sound of the Sultan's entry, the young man raised his tear-stained face and, after exchanging greetings with the visitor, said, 'Sire, pray pardon me for not rising to greet you.'

With that he buried his head in his hands and wept as if his heart would break.

Much surprised, the Sultan gently asked the reason for his grief.

'How can I not weep when this is my state?' he replied.

So saying, he lifted up his robe, revealing a body turned to marble from the waist down to the feet.

'My poor friend,' said the Sultan, 'how is it you are like other men from the waist up to the head, yet made of stone below the waist?'

'I will tell you, sire,' said he. 'My father was Mahmud, King of this palace and the four black islands. The four hills hereabouts were once black islands and the lake was the capital of our realm. After a long reign of seventy years, my father died and I succeeded to the throne; soon after I took a wife, my cousin, whom I dearly loved. She loved me too, so much that if I had to be away she would neither eat nor drink till my return.

'Five years passed. Then, one day, when my wife was out and I was dozing in the afternoon heat, fanned by two slave girls, I heard one tell the other how sad it was that I was married to an unfaithful wife. The other agreed, saying my wife was an enchantress who drugged me each night with wine before stealing off to her master to dabble in black arts.

'As I listened to this conversation with my eyes shut, though my spirit was wide awake, the light turned to darkness before my mind's eye, and I could hardly wait for nightfall to test whether what I had heard was true. When my wife, therefore, handed me a goblet of wine as usual, I turned my face from her and, pretending to drink, poured it away. I then lay down and feigned a heavy sleep.

'At that I heard my wife say, "Sleep on and never wake. By Allah, how I hate you!"

'She then arose, dressed herself in her best robes and left the room. Silently, I followed as she made her way out of the palace, through the streets and down to the city gates; there she uttered some magic words and the iron gates opened by themselves. On and on she walked until she arrived at a small mud hut standing all alone. When she had entered I climbed upon the roof so that I could see through a hole what transpired within.

'What I saw, O Sultan, was my wife kissing the ground before an ugly old wizard who treated her worse than a slave: he threw her rat bones to gnaw and abused her most horribly. Yet she worshipped him. Finally, I could bear it no longer and, breaking into the hut, I took out

'Sleep on and never
wake . . .'

*He picked up
the corpse
and threw it
down a well.*

my sword and went to cut off the villain's head. But in my fury I only wounded him before I made my escape, undetected by my wife.

'Next morning I noticed that my wife had cut off her hair and put on her mourning clothes; she told me she had had news of her mother's death. Showing compassion, I told her to do what she thought fitting; she continued thus to weep and mourn for an entire year, after which she told me she wished to build a tomb within the palace where she might go to mourn each day. She was to call it the tomb of sorrow.

'Having received my assent, she had a grand tomb built into which she moved the wounded wizard. After my sword blow he had lost his magic power and was very weak, yet he did not die. Now my wife was able to tend to him all the time: she visited him every day, early and late, to nurse his wound and mourn over him, feeding him with the choicest foods. Patiently I suffered for another year until one day I entered her apartment unawares to find her slapping her face and crying, "My heart loves none but you; should you die I would lie beside you in your grave. And if I die, then speak my name above my grave, and my bones shall answer to your call."

'The moment she finished her lament, I rushed in, sword drawn, intent on killing her for her infidelity – for I had lost patience at last.

'But just as I was about to strike the blow, she pronounced some magic word that made me as you see now: half-stone, half-man, half-dead and half-alive. That done, the evil woman submerged the city beneath a lake and turned the four races of the city into fish: Muslims white, Magians red, Christians blue and Jews yellowish-brown. Further, she changed the four black islands into hills around the lake.

'That is not all. Every day she comes to torment me, giving me a hundred lashes with a leather thong, so that the blood flows down my wounded back.'

At the end of his story, the tormented Prince wept without cease.

'My poor man,' the Sultan said to soothe him, much moved by what he'd heard, 'and where, pray, is this woman now?'

'She will be here for certain at the crack of dawn to whip me and tend to her wizard,' he said.

Since it would soon be dawn, the Sultan rose and went straight to the tomb of sorrow where the wizard lay. With a blow of his sword, the Sultan killed what little life remained within the man, picked up his corpse and threw it down a well. Returning to the tomb, he clothed himself in the wizard's garb, blew out all the candles so that it was dark inside the tomb, then lay down upon the couch, his drawn sword by his side, ready and waiting.

Soon after, the wicked wife arrived, whipped her poor half-stone husband a hundred times, then came into the darkened tomb.

'O my master,' she cried, 'how do you feel today?'

At her voice the Sultan spoke in muffled tones: 'How can I feel well

when your husband's cries disturb my peace? Return him to his proper shape and give me rest.'

'To hear is to obey, O master,' said the wife; immediately she rose and went into her husband's room. Taking a cup of water she said some words above it, then sprinkled the lower half of her husband's body with drops of water. He instantly regained his former shape.

'Now get out of my sight before I kill you,' she screamed at him before returning to the tomb.

'O master, the disturber of your peace is gone,' she cried to her beloved.

In a feeble voice, the Sultan murmured, 'You have removed the branch but not the root. The people of the four black islands give me no peace: every night, at the middle hour, the fish raise their heads and cry vengeance on us both. If you restore them all, my strength will no doubt return.'

On hearing these words, she sprang up, full of joy, and hastened to the lake where she pronounced some magic words above its waters. At once the fish raised their heads and were turned into humans once again: Muslims and Christians, Magians and Jews. The city reappeared from the lake, with its streets and houses, bustling markets and dusty bazaars; and the hills crumbled into islands as before.

That done, the enchantress hurried back to the tomb, crying, 'It is done, O master, as you wished.'

'Approach and kiss my hand,' the Sultan commanded.

So she drew near and, all of a sudden, received a sharp sword thrust into her bosom, so hard that it went right through her and out the other side. To make sure she was dead, the Sultan withdrew the blade and, with a mighty blow, cut her right in two.

Then he went to the young man and told him his evil wife was dead.

'Now,' said the Sultan, 'I must return to my own city; how fortunate that it is so close to yours.'

The young Prince frowned. 'Your realm is a whole year's journey hence,' he said. 'You only came here so swiftly because you were enchanted. However, I shall go with you, since you have saved my life.'

The Sultan was delighted to have the young Prince as companion.

'Praise be to Allah,' he cried; 'and since I have no children I shall make you my son and heir.'

They embraced and set off on the journey home, overladen with gifts from the Prince's palace. It was almost a year before they drew near the Sultan's city; and there they were met with great rejoicing by the Grand Vizier and the Sultan's army that had been left behind. When all things were settled, the Sultan said to his Vizier, 'Fetch the fisherman here; it was he who first presented me with the fish, so he is the real saviour of the sunken realm.'

When the old fisherman appeared, the Sultan enquired whether he was lucky enough to have any children.

'I have two daughters and a son,' the fisherman replied.

On hearing this, the Sultan did the old man the honour of marrying one of his daughters himself, and wedded the other to the handsome Prince. Meanwhile, the son was made the Sultan's treasurer. As for the fisherman, he became one of the wealthiest people of his age and his proud descendants along the coast of Syria still bear his name.

Nor was the young Prince's land left without a monarch: the faithful Vizier was sent to rule the four black islands, and this he did justly and wisely to the end of his days.

'Approach and kiss my hand,' the Sultan commanded.

Sinbad the Sailor

N THE GOLDEN AGE OF THE CALIPH Haroon Al-Rashid, in the city of Baghdad, there was a wealthy merchant named Sinbad; he made so many voyages across the sea that folk called him Sinbad the Sailor.

This is the story of some of his wonderful adventures.

One time, he set sail from the port of Basrah and crossed many seas, trading in each land he reached. After a long voyage, the master of the ship cast anchor alongside an island as green and pleasant as the gardens of paradise. In the company of all the crew, Sinbad went ashore to stretch his legs and explore the island. Some sailors set to lighting fires and cooking food, others washed and scrubbed their linen, yet others played games with a horse-hair ball.

Amidst this calm and gaiety, the ship's master suddenly shouted in alarm, 'Run for your lives! Back to the ship! Quick! Quick!'

The island was moving . . .

Some sailors managed to reach the ship, hauled up the anchor as swiftly as they could and sailed off on the wind. But Sinbad and several other mariners were left stranded on the shore as the island heaved and bucked, then sank beneath the foaming waves.

In truth, what they had thought was an island was really a huge whale which had slept so long that an entire island had grown upon its back, with palm trees and bushes, feather grass and wild flowers. The sea monster had obviously been rudely woken by the fires; and in its pain had dived to the bottom of the sea along with pots and pans, half-cooked dinners and drowning sailors.

So Sinbad found himself struggling in the choppy, churned-up sea, bobbing up and down amid planks and spars and bits of trees. As luck would have it, he was saved from drowning by a wooden washtub that floated by his head; he quickly scrambled in and, using his feet as paddles, steered himself clear of the seething whirlpool above the sunken island. Meanwhile, he watched in desperation as his ship disappeared beyond the watery horizon.

He was sure he would die as the ocean tossed him like a piece of

flotsam to and fro into the open sea. Night fell, and he was engulfed in darkness. Then, miraculously, the next day a fresh breeze drove him and his washtub within sight of another shore. This land was certainly no sea monster: it had cliffs towering above the beach and tall trees overhanging its little bay. As he drifted towards the shore, Sinbad managed to grab an overhanging branch and pull himself on to dry land.

Half-drowned, the poor castaway pitched face-forward on to the warm sand. His legs were numb and bleeding, nibbled by the fish that had attacked him on the way. Faint from fatigue, he remained senseless on the shore till dawn the next day. Then, warmed by the morning sun, Sinbad awoke and crawled up the sand to a fresh-water spring; there he drank greedily and washed his blood-stained legs. Refreshed, he glanced about him and noticed trees heavy with sweet fruits to eat. So

he ate his fill and, in the course of several days, revived his body and his spirit enough to walk about.

He explored the entire island, finding it empty of humans, yet full of many friendly creatures and leafy trees. With strength renewed, Sinbad decided to make himself a little hut of broad palm leaves, and began taming a flock of goats to provide him with milk and meat. The days passed into months then, one day, as the stranded mariner was leaning on his staff upon the cliffs, gazing out to sea, he spotted the white sails of a ship. With fast-beating heart, he watched it sail into the bay, cast anchor and let out a landing plank.

How surprised the captain was to find the ragged castaway upon the island; gladly he brought the man aboard and listened to his tale. When Sinbad asked him about his cargo and port of destination, the captain replied, 'I have a cargo of merchandise in my hold; but its owner,

The days passed into months, then one day, as the stranded mariner was gazing out to sea . . .

41

God rest his soul, went down with an island that sank into the sea. A most amazing tale. I am going to sell his wares and take the money to his widow.'

'And where did this man live?' asked Sinbad.

'At Baghdad, the abode of peace,' the captain replied.

In growing excitement, Sinbad then asked, 'And what, pray, was his name?'

'Sinbad the Sailor,' was the reply.

'Captain,' cried Sinbad with joy, 'do you not know me? It is I, Sinbad. I am the merchant of whom you speak.'

Thereupon he told the story of his strange escape in such detail there could be no doubt he was who he claimed he was. The honest captain, who at first thought the man out to get his hands on Sinbad's goods, was soon convinced, and he embraced the merchant who had returned from the dead.

So Sinbad the Sailor sailed with the crew for home. Fortune, however, decided otherwise. Sinbad was not destined to reach the port of Basrah or the abode of peace on that voyage. This is what came to pass on the way.

On the way home the ship had put in at an island for fresh water and provisions. It was a large island with fig and date trees heavy with ripe fruit; there were blossoming flowers of heady fragrance, crystal-clear streams and fountains and cheery birdsong. On landing, Sinbad set forth alone to explore the lovely island, eat some figs and drink from the pure cool fountains. He sat down to rest beside a palm tree; in no time at all he had fallen into the sweetest slumber.

How long he slept he did not know. But when he awoke he found that he was alone, the ship had gone, and not a soul remained. His shipmates had forgotten all about him in their eagerness to get home.

In despair, Sinbad sank to the sandy shore and wept. Lightning did not strike in the same place twice; nor could he hope to be rescued a second time by a calling ship. He was surely doomed to spend the remainder of his days upon this lonely island.

After he had used up all his tears, he rose slowly to his feet and walked about the island. To gain a better view of his new home he climbed a lofty tree and peered around: there was nothing there except sky and water, trees and birds, rocks and sand. However, in the distance a white object caught his eye. So he clambered down the tree and walked towards it, eventually arriving at an enormous oval dome with no door or window for an entrance. It was too smooth to climb and, when Sinbad had walked right round it, he found it full fifty paces from start to end.

42

*It was too smooth to climb and
full fifty paces from start to end.*

The day was drawing to a close as Sinbad puzzled over this giant
house, when suddenly he felt the sky grow dark and a shadow fell upon
the ground. Looking up he saw a giant bird with wide flapping wings
and a beak as huge as a sailing ship. He at once remembered a sailors'
tale about monster birds called rocs which lived on certain islands in
the ocean and fed their young on elephants. No doubt about it: the white
oval dome was a giant roc's egg!

As Sinbad quickly hid among the trees, the huge bird flew down and
landed on the egg, covering it with its body like a brooding hen.

While he watched in awe, a desperate plan formed in Sinbad's head:
perhaps the roc flew to other islands on which there might be humans;
if he were to fly with it, somehow he might yet escape his lonely fate.

Unwinding the turban from his head, he tied one end about his waist
and then, approaching the sleeping roc on tiptoe, he tied the other to
one of the bird's legs.

All night long he waited, not daring to sleep and holding tight to the
roc's scaly leg. Then at dawn the bird let forth a squawk and rose up

Sinbad's heart was in his mouth
as he clung tightly to the roc.

into the sky; it did not notice its passenger at all. Sinbad's heart was in his mouth as he clung tightly to the roc, which swooped and soared through the air; eventually it dived down to earth and landed gently on a rocky plain. Hastily, he unwound his turban from the scaly leg and, shaking in every limb, scampered away to safety. From behind a rock, he watched in horror as the giant bird pounced upon a huge squirming serpent as long as a minaret. Seizing the serpent in its talons, the roc flew off across the sea, squawking happily.

As soon as the bird had gone, Sinbad came out of hiding and set off to explore the plain; to his anguish he found he was in the foothills of a barren mountain that almost touched the sky. Before him stretched an endless desert valley with neither trees, nor pools, nor grass. He now began to regret having left the bountiful island: at least he had had plenty there to eat and drink. Every time he escaped from one fate he seemed to suffer an even greater calamity.

Sinbad started to make his way across the plain and, to his amazement, found that the rocky land was strewn with diamonds glittering in the sun. But that was not all he found. For the plain was also full of hissing snakes, each one thicker than a palm tree and fat enough to eat an elephant.

Fearing to be gobbled up by a snake, Sinbad kept close to the mountain edge. All of a sudden, he had an awful shock, for right beside him, with a crash, fell the carcass of a sheep. Glancing up and shielding his eyes against the sun, he tried to catch a glimpse of whoever it was that had tossed the sheep upon the ground.

Then he remembered. He had heard a story long ago about a valley of diamonds guarded by hordes of snakes; of how hunters would toss fresh meat down the mountainside to stick to the diamonds. And if they were lucky, vultures would then swoop upon the meat, fly with it to the mountain top where hunters would be waiting with gongs and bells to scare them off. That way the men would be able to get the diamonds.

That gave Sinbad an idea.

Filling his pockets, turban and robes with as many gems as he could, he crawled underneath the dead carcass of the sheep and clung on tightly to its fleece. After what seemed an age, he heard the flapping of wings and felt himself being borne aloft to the mountain top, where he was dropped with a bump upon the ground. All at once a great clatter and howling went up behind him, frightening away the vulture.

Imagine the fright Sinbad gave the hunters when they came to claim their prize. But he quickly calmed their fears as he told the story of his escape and shared his diamonds with the men. Then he accompanied the hunters as they crossed mountains and valleys, finally arriving at a busy port where he joined a ship sailing for Basrah. Before leaving for home he exchanged some of his diamonds for gold and silver and a great wealth of merchandise. Then off he sailed.

*The ship crashed against the rocks
and soon the rigging was
swarming with black hairy apes.*

There were several other merchants on board the sailing ship, all
excited by the prospect of good fortune and trade across the seas. At first
the voyage went well, the ship putting in from port to port, island to
island, land to land. And at each port of call the merchants bought new
wares and sold at twice the price; all were therefore in good spirits.

Then one day, as they sailed amidst a tempestuous sea, the ship
heaved and creaked, and the captain called above the storm that all was
lost: the wind had driven them off course and they were heading for the
island of the apes. It was not long before the ship crashed against some
rocks and, in next to no time, the rigging swarmed with black hairy
apes with red gleaming eyes and long rat-like tails. They were just like a
plague of locusts as they clambered up the mast and stays, biting through
the ropes and cables and gathering up the cargo. Then, seizing all the
merchants and crew, they made off with them to their island; next, to the
men's surprise, they were rudely dumped upon the shore as the
monkeys ran off with the merchandise.

With the ship slowly sinking in the stormy sea, the men watched
helplessly from the shore; there was nothing they could do. At last, they
set off inland, meaning to explore the island of the apes. It was not long

47

before they came in sight of a tall pavilion, its iron gates wide open. All the men entered, finding themselves within a wide dusty courtyard; in the centre was a giant cauldron hung above a smouldering fire. Everywhere were piles of bones picked clean and parched white in the sun.

There was no sign of life about the place.

The men, being hungry, helped themselves to fresh water from the well, figs and dates from the trees lining the walls, and took their ease. Thus it continued until sunset when, all of a sudden, the earth trembled, a roaring rent the air, and a giant black ape came into the yard. The men had never set eyes on a sight more hideous: the ape was as tall as the highest palm tree, as black as the darkest night, as hairy as a coconut. His two eyes blazed with fire, his thick lips hung down like a camel's, his huge sharp teeth chattered like a thousand drums, and his black tail swung to and fro like that of a lion in a cage.

When the men saw him, they cowered together in a corner of the yard, frozen with fright. The giant ape advanced and, bending down, seized Sinbad between finger and thumb, lifting him high above the ground and inspecting him from top to toe, as a butcher would a lamb for roasting. Evidently finding Sinbad too lean, the giant set him down again. This procedure continued with Sinbad's companions until the ape seized the master of the ship who was strong and stout.

Thereupon, the black beast grunted in satisfaction, dashed the squirming body to the ground, stepped on it with one massive paw and tore off its head. Then, fetching a spit, he hung the body above the fire to roast, turning it continually so that it was evenly cooked. When the ape thought it ready, he tore off joints as one would from a chicken and swallowed them down until only a few bones remained.

Then the giant ape lay down to sleep, his snores rumbling in his throat like the death-rattle of a slaughtered beast. At dawn he rose and ambled away.

As soon as he had gone, the men began to confer together, wishing they had been drowned in the sea on their way to the island; anything was better than being killed and roasted on a spit by that monster. There was no escape, for the iron gates had swung to and were firmly locked from the outside, and the walls were too high and smooth to be scaled. All day long the men bewailed their fate; then, at sunset, they were terrified to feel the ground and air tremble about them as the big black beast approached.

Once again the ape felt each man between finger and thumb before selecting one to his taste. That victim met the same fate as the master of the ship: he was dashed to the ground, stamped on, his head was torn off, he was skewered on a spit, roasted and eaten.

After the giant had dined and belched more than once to express his satisfaction, he lay down to sleep, rattling and wheezing like a raging

48

storm. And once more at dawn he rose and went away.

As soon as the beast was gone, the men all crowded round Sinbad who had thought up a plan.

'If we stay here,' he said, 'we will be roasted and eaten one by one. We must somehow kill this beast and escape; we can make rafts and put to sea. Likely as not we shall drown, but even that is a sweeter fate than staying here.'

To this they all agreed.

So, when evening came and the ogre rushed at them like a snarling dog, picked a victim, ate him then went to sleep, the men were ready. They prepared two iron rods, heated them in the fire until they were red hot, then, grasping the ends firmly, they ran full tilt at the giant ape, thrusting the glowing ends into his eyes with all their force.

At once he let out a deafening bellow, jumped up and down, and lashed about to left and right. But the men had pressed themselves against the courtyard walls to avoid being hurt. Finally, the ape crashed into the iron gates and, with one push, knocked them flat, stumbling down to the sea to cool his burning face.

The men followed at a distance, but the ogre-ape had disappeared. At once each mariner set to feverishly making his own raft. Just as they were finishing this task, however, the ground suddenly shook more violently than before and, looking up in alarm, they beheld a terrifying

They sank every single raft except one – Sinbad's.

sight: the ape was returning with what was evidently his wife, even bigger and more hideous than him.

As quickly as they could, the men launched their clumsy rafts and paddled off as fast as their strength would allow. But the two apes hurled rocks after them and sank every single raft, drowning their occupants. All but one. For Sinbad had managed to paddle out of reach, even though rocks had fallen all around him. Thanking Allah for his escape, the exhausted sailor fell asleep upon his raft and drifted across the sea.

How long he travelled thus he did not know, but when he awoke he was overjoyed to see a passing ship. He quickly hailed it, and was taken on board to safety. He was dressed in warm clothes, fed and revived, though, truth to tell, no one believed his astounding tale.

But Sinbad, it seems, was a harbinger of ill luck. For not long after, his new vessel keeled over in a storm and went to the bottom with its cargo.

However, once again, Sinbad's charmed life saved him from a watery grave. Clinging to a plank from the ship, he was tossed by wind and waves until he was cast upon a sandy shore. And there he slept until the morning sun warmed his back and gently nursed him back to life.

He pulled himself to his feet, staggered up the sand and set out to explore his new home. He had not gone far when, to his surprise – for it

did not occur to him that he was not alone – he saw an old man sitting by a stream. He looked an odd old fellow with his straggly hair and white hanging beard; he was naked except for a skirt of banana leaves.

'Hello there, shipmate,' Sinbad called. 'How come you here?'

There was no answer. Instead, the old man shook his head and sighed, signalling to Sinbad to carry him across the stream. Mindful of a place reserved in heaven for those who help the poor, Sinbad took him upon his shoulders and waded through the shallow stream until he reached the bank.

Yet when he went to set down the old man from his back, he found he would not budge. No matter what Sinbad did he could not shake off the old man. The fellow twisted his legs round Sinbad's neck and sat astride his shoulders. Each time Sinbad tried to dislodge him, he squeezed hard on Sinbad's throat so he could not breathe. And every time the poor sailor sank to his knees, nearly fainting from lack of air, the old man struck him with a stick; the pain forced Sinbad to his feet and on his way. With hefty blows upon the back and shoulders, the old man directed Sinbad to right and left, back and forth, just like a clumsy mule.

Thus it was that Sinbad had to carry his unwelcome load wherever the old man wished to go; and if he dragged his feet or stopped to catch his breath, the old man beat him without mercy. Sinbad became his slave.

The old man did not dismount by night or day; whenever he wished to sleep he would wind his legs even tighter round Sinbad's neck and doze – at which poor Sinbad would take the opportunity to rest a little too. But such respite never lasted for long. The old man would soon awake and set to beating his bearer even more.

How Sinbad cursed his charity. Sometimes a good deed can turn sour.

So it went on for days and weeks and months, until one day Sinbad was driven to a spot where pumpkins grew. As the old man was slumbering, Sinbad picked a pumpkin that was big and dry, cleaned it out and filled it with juice which he squeezed from grapes. This he left in the sun for several days until it turned to wine; each morning thereafter, as the old man slept, Sinbad took a gulp of wine to help him through the day.

Not long after, the old man opened his eyes just as Sinbad was drinking from the pumpkin bowl. He made a sign as if asking what the liquid was, to which Sinbad honestly replied, 'It freshens my heart and gives me strength.'

To demonstrate, Sinbad took a deep draught of wine and ran off with the old devil still on his back, danced among the trees, clapped his hands, giggled and sang.

When the old man saw Sinbad in that state, he made signs towards

With a sudden tilt forward,
he sent the old man
crashing to the ground.

the pumpkin and his own mouth, whereupon Sinbad gave it to him to drink. Greedily, he drained the pumpkin dry. All and every drop.

In no time at all, his eyes began to roll, his shoulders shook and his arms flapped loosely about. As his legs loosened their grip, Sinbad seized his chance.

With a sudden tilt forward, he sent the old man crashing to the ground – and there he lay in a drunken sleep. Sinbad could scarcely believe he was free, though he feared the old man would rise again and torment him if he could. So he picked up a large rock and brought it crashing down on the old man's skull. His tormentor was dead.

With a light heart Sinbad wandered about the island, eating sweet fruit and drinking from the crystal streams, keeping a constant watch for a passing ship. But he was out of luck. The months and then the years rolled by in lonely desperation. He wondered often whether he would ever see his family again, and he vowed that if he was saved he would never go to sea again.

His dear wife was overjoyed to see him again.

Then one stormy day, when he had given up all hope, he suddenly spied a sailing ship being tossed about in the angry sea. It had to take refuge in his island bay until the storm had ceased.

So Sinbad was saved again.

When he was aboard and had told his story to the captain of the ship, the good man said, 'You are a very lucky man. That old fellow who rode upon your back was the old man of the sea; he is much feared by mariners. No shipwrecked sailor has ever escaped from him before. Praise be to Allah for your safety.'

Sinbad was brought food and new clothing, but his heart was heavy. For he had a sad foreboding that he would bring misfortune upon these good sailors, just as he had on all the others. But this time the fair wind of fortune was with the ship and the voyage was calm and uneventful.

Several weeks later he arrived back in his dear Baghdad at last. After thanking the captain and the crew, Sinbad made his way home with some uncertainty. After all, many years had passed since he last set foot there. Would his family still be alive? Would they remember him? Would his wife have married again?

He need have had no fears.

True, his children were all grown up, and many of his older relations had died. But his dear wife, who naturally had thought him dead, was overjoyed to see him again. How much rejoicing there was in Sinbad's household – with all his family and friends about him. And in the course of the celebrations Sinbad the Sailor told the amazing story of his adventures.

So wonderful was his tale that it finally reached the ears of the Caliph himself, who summoned the wanderer and had his story written down for all posterity.

And when the length of Sinbad's travels was calculated, from the first to the last adventure, it was found to be full twenty-seven years.

The Flying Horse

HERE WAS IN ANCIENT TIMES, in the city of Sheeraz in Persia, a mighty Shah who had three daughters as lovely as the shining sun. And he had a son as pale and handsome as the moon.

It was the custom of Shah Shapoor to open up his palace to his subjects at the annual Festival of Now-roz. The Shah being fascinated by science and geometry, nothing pleased him more than one of his subjects bringing some new mechanical device to show him, some wonderful invention to demonstrate.

One year, at the time of the Now-roz Festival, three men came forward with their gifts: a golden peacock, a brass trumpet and a horse of ebony.

'Tell me how they work,' said the Shah, his curiosity aroused.

'My peacock will flap its wings and squawk to tell the time on every hour of the day and night,' explained its proud inventor.

'My trumpet will sound whenever an enemy approaches,' declared its owner.

'And my horse will take a man wherever he desires,' the man with the horse said.

The Shah was delighted. 'If your inventions are as wonderful as you claim,' he said, 'I shall grant you any reward you ask.'

With that he tried out the peacock and found the man was telling the truth. He tried out the trumpet and found it as its owner said.

'Ask and your wishes will be fulfilled,' the Shah then declared.

Each man requested one of the Shah's lovely daughters for his wife; and their wishes were granted. Thereupon, the man with the ebony horse came forward and claimed the same reward.

'First I must put your invention to the test,' the monarch replied.

'Father, let me be the first to try it,' cried the Shah's son, stepping forward.

At a nod from the Shah, the master of the ebony horse showed the young Prince a peg in the hollow of the horse's wooden neck. 'By turning the peg, the horse will fly into the air,' said the inventor.

Even before anyone could move, the Prince had eagerly mounted the magic horse, turned the peg and soared up into the sky. Soon horse and rider had disappeared from sight, leaving the Shah and his subjects gazing forlornly after him.

However, as the Prince soon realized to his dismay, he did not know how to arrest his mount's ascent, nor how to bring it back to earth. As he examined every portion of the flying horse, the only things he came across were two wooden cock's heads on either side of the horse's neck. Nothing more.

So he tried turning the cock's head on the right and at once flew upwards swiftly; then he turned the one on the left, at which the horse began descending gently. Now that he knew how to control the horse, the Prince flew up and down at will throughout the day, enjoying the wonderful sights on land and sea and in the clear blue sky. He looked down on many lands he did not know until at last he found himself flying above a splendid city set like a pearl inside a crown. He flew round and round this city, viewing it from every side.

The day being late and the sun about to set, the Prince decided to pass the night within this place, bringing down the horse upon the flat roof of a splendid palace. Not knowing what people lived within, he prudently waited until the dark of night when all were, as he thought, in bed. Then, feeling hungry, he crept down a staircase into a marble courtyard leading off to various halls and chambers.

Everywhere was silent and deserted.

Puzzled, he was about to return to his horse when he saw a light approaching through the gloom. A party of young girls appeared, and in their midst was a lovely damsel, tall and slender like an iris, of whom the poet said,

> *She came without a call in the dark of night,*
> *Like a full moon in the darkened sky.*
> *Of slender form, there is none in all creation like her*
> *In the graceful way she walks.*

So thought the young Prince as he gazed upon her.

The damsel was the Princess of Bengal, eldest daughter of the Rajah, who loved her so much that he had had the splendid summer palace built for her amusement. Thus, when her spirit was low she would come there in the company of her maids and play games, sing and dance, and lighten her soul. As now it was.

Concealing himself behind the curtains while the party danced and played their games, the young Prince looked on, entranced. But he grew careless and did not notice his shadow falling on the wall; it was seen by a serving maid who at once let out a shriek. Realizing he was found out, the Prince stepped forward and fell on his knees before the lovely Princess of Bengal.

'Dear lady,' he said, 'by the most extraordinary adventure you see

the son of the Shah of Persia before you. When I return to my land, I shall leave my heart behind, for your grace and beauty have stolen it from my breast.'

'I am afraid,' the Princess sighed, 'that when my father hears of this he will be very angry and have you put to death. You see, dear Prince, I am promised to an old and ugly rajah; and by our law any man who sets eyes on me before my marriage has to die.'

Despite her entreaties to him to leave by the way he came, the Prince vowed he would not desert her. Could she not fly away with him? After all, she clearly did not love the ugly rajah. After much imploring, the Princess finally agreed. And, having her maids adorn her head, neck, arms and waist with the largest diamonds in her treasure-chest, she put on a royal blue sari of the finest silk.

As the first rays of dawn were streaking through the sky, the young pair climbed up the staircase to the palace roof and mounted the ebony horse, the Prince in front, the Princess behind, clinging to his waist. Then, with a turn of the wooden peg, they soared up into the dawning sky, flying back the way the Prince had come. And within the space of half a day the Prince had guided the magic horse back to the city of Sheeraz.

Now, while the Prince had been away, his father, fearful that he had flown up to the sun and burnt to death, had punished the horse's master for his carelessness: he had had the man whipped soundly and sent away without reward. So the horse's inventor had lost his flying horse and been whipped into the bargain.

Each day he raised his tired eyes to the sky, searching for his horse's return. And at last his patience was rewarded. For he spied the Prince and Princess of Bengal descending into a garden of the Shah's summer palace, some way from the town. The Prince, wishing to convey the news of his safe return and new bride to his father himself, had landed, as he thought, in secret. Now he left the Princess and the horse in the garden and hurried off to inform the Shah.

Now was the inventor's chance. Eager to take revenge for his suffering and to seize back his magic horse, he hastened to the palace garden and presented himself to the Princess as an envoy of the Prince.

'He has sent me to fetch you on the flying horse,' the inventor said, bowing low before her. 'Mount up behind me and I shall fly you to him.'

Unsuspecting, the lovely Bengal maid climbed up behind the old inventor, eager to be together with her Prince.

Up into the air they flew as the inventor turned the cock's head peg upon the horse's neck; they flew low over the rooftops of the city, so that their shadow fell across the town. As the Princess looked down she suddenly saw the Shah and Prince, attended by a splendid host of courtiers, riding along the road towards the summer palace she had just left. It was then she realized she had been tricked.

With a wicked laugh of triumph, the inventor swooped low above their heads, showing off his prize and taunting the Shah and his son.

The long retinue halted, all eyes turned upwards in amazement and dismay. But there was nothing anyone could do; even if an archer fired an arrow it might easily mean death for the poor Princess. The broken-hearted Prince returned to the palace in despair, as the horse soared high into the sky and disappeared.

They flew low over the rooftops of the city.

*At once the Sultan rode
towards the maiden's cries.*

Although the Princess wept and begged, the inventor was unmoved.

'The Shah refused to give me his daughter as my wife; instead he had me flogged. This is his punishment and my revenge. Henceforth you will be my wife and I your master.'

Despite her tears and pleas, the inventor flew his magic horse on and on throughout the day and night until next day, at dawn, he landed in a wood within the kingdom of Kashmir. Tying the Princess to a tree, he went off to fetch some food to eat. On his return he untied the maid, shouting at her roughly, 'Now cook some breakfast or I'll beat you till you're black and blue.'

But maids of Bengal are not as meek as their Persian sisters, and the Princess spat full in his face.

'I would rather die than cook for you or be your wife,' she shouted back at him.

True to his threat, the inventor took up a stick and set to beating her violently. Luckily, though, as she screamed in pain her cries were heard by someone close at hand. It so happened that the Sultan of Kashmir and his party were out hunting in the wood not far from the wooden horse. At once the Sultan rode towards the maiden's cries; finding the couple he addressed the Princess's tormentor: 'Why do you treat this lady so cruelly? Has she been untrue?'

'Sire,' the inventor exclaimed, cross at the intrusion, 'I am her master, she my wife. I treat her therefore as I will. It is no business of yours.'

The Princess, who knew neither the rank nor intentions of her would-be rescuer, begged for help.

'My lord,' she cried, 'heaven must have sent you to save me. I am the Princess of Bengal, eldest daughter of the Rajah there; this old tormentor stole me away from my intended husband, the Prince of Persia; he brought me here upon his flying horse against my will and he whips me now because I will not become his wife.'

The Princess hardly had need of words: her royal grace and bearing proclaimed she spoke the truth, even though her fine robe was torn. Enraged at the insolent and cruel inventor, the Sultan had him seized and lashed until he breathed no more; then he had his head chopped off.

Thereupon the Sultan had the Princess taken to his palace with the magic horse: the horse was deposited in his treasury, while the maid was taken to a magnificent chamber next to the Sultan's room and given a host of serving maids to attend to her every need. How happy she was at being saved from the evil inventor; she was sure the Sultan would soon complete his kindness by returning her to her beloved Prince.

But her hopes were rudely dashed. For the Sultan's intention was to add her to his harem of wives – he did not have a dusky Bengal maid amongst them. Thus, as the poor Princess awoke next morning, she heard the sound of drums and trumpets, announcing the wedding-to-

be. And when she heard the news, she was plunged once more into despair. However, the Princess was made of stubborn stuff and firmly refused to break her promise to the Persian Prince, the sole man that she loved. Yet how was she to put off the Sultan?

At last she worked out a plan: she would pretend to be mad.

Thus it was, as the Sultan next approached, she threw herself upon the floor, shrieking and kicking like someone demented. She tore at her long black tresses, scratched her face and arms, even pretending to attack the Sultan, trying to tear him to shreds with her sharp fingernails.

When he found her in such a frenzy, the Sultan was most distressed; he commended her to her serving maids, bidding them take good care of her and make her better. He came to see her every day, hoping she would soon be cured. But instead her madness grew worse. She gibbered and acted like a wild beast, so finally the Sultan sent for the best doctors in the land to find a cure.

'He who can cure the Princess will receive a munificent reward,' it was announced.

Doctors came from far and wide to try their skill, but none met with success.

In the meantime, while a cure was being sought, the grieving Shah's son had donned the simple cloak of a dervish and set out to seek his lost Princess. He wandered through many lands until one day, while

She sprang at him snarling like a wild beast.

passing through a famous city in Hindustan, he heard some merchants in the bazaar talking about a certain Princess of Bengal: it seemed that she had turned violently mad on the very day of her intended wedding to the Sultan of Kashmir. And though doctors had tried to cure her, none had so far managed to make her sane. The merchants went on to talk of the inventor's fate and of the flying horse that now stood within the Sultan's treasury, since none knew how to work it.

The Prince was overjoyed: not only was he sure this was his beloved Princess, but also that she had feigned madness to keep her vow to him.

So he journeyed to the kingdom of Kashmir and came to the palace, where he announced his wish to try to cure the mad Princess. Since his beard was long and his simple dervish's cloak gave him the appearance of a holy man, he was easily taken for the character he assumed and was permitted to try a cure.

The Sultan warned him that all other doctors and holy men had failed; some, indeed, had had their eyes scratched out by the wild woman's nails.

While the Sultan watched and listened from behind a lattice window, the bearded dervish was let into the Princess's room. As soon as she set eyes on him – taking him to be yet another fortune-seeker – she screamed and kicked and scratched, threw herself upon the floor, then sprang at him snarling like a wild beast, as if to tear out his eyes.

Boldly he stepped towards the Princess and when he was near enough for her, and no one else, to hear, he murmured, 'My Princess, I am not a dervish, but the Prince of Persia, come to save you. Take me for what I am, not what I seem.'

She recognized his voice at once and was overwhelmed with joy at seeing the man she had awaited for so long. But, aware of the Sultan's eyes upon her, she groaned and trembled as if in agony, now and then slipping out a phrase in low tones between her screams. In such manner the two conversed, declaring their love anew and working out a plan. They plotted that after his visit the Princess would act more calmly and would consent to see the Sultan on the morrow.

The Sultan was, of course, delighted with the news and the apparent change in his intended bride.

'But I have not cured her completely,' the Prince-dervish said. 'She has a demon inside her that I must drive out. Tell me, O wise Sultan, how did she come to Kashmir, since her native land is so far away?'

And the Sultan told the story of the wooden horse; it seemed to be enchanted, though no one knew exactly how it worked.

'Ah, I see,' the dervish said. 'I think I know the cure then. Since the Princess was brought here on that magic horse, she must be possessed by some enchantment from it. If you, O Sultan, would wish to treat your court and townsfolk to a truly astonishing sight, have the horse brought tomorrow into the palace square, and leave the rest to me. I promise to show you the Princess entirely well in mind and body. And one more thing: have the Princess dressed in the most costly silks and gems.'

The Sultan was ready to do anything to cure the lovely Princess so he could wed her, and he eagerly agreed.

Next day, the flying horse was taken from the treasury and placed in the palace square; the news had quickly spread throughout the town and an enormous crowd now thronged the square. So many people were there that the guards had trouble keeping a free space around the horse. Meanwhile, the Sultan and all his nobles sat up in a gallery overlooking the palace square.

At an order from the dervish, the Princess of Bengal, richly dressed and bejewelled, was led out quietly from her room and set upon the horse. As she was seated upon its back, the Prince-dervish lit small fires all about the horse and cast some purple powder into each; at once they gave off dense clouds of smoke which enveloped the ebony horse and the Princess.

With a nimble leap, the Prince suddenly sprang upon the horse in front of his dear Princess. And as she put her arms tightly about his waist, he quickly turned the cock's head peg. To gasps of amazement from the crowd, the horse, the Prince and the Princess rose up, up, up into the air and flew away across the town. And as they flew, the Prince's words were plainly heard upon the breeze.

'Sultan of Kashmir,' he called, 'if you ever wish to marry a Princess who seeks your protection, make sure you ask her permission first!'

And off they flew to Persia. It was not long before they alighted in the palace courtyard, right before the delighted Shah. That very day a magnificent wedding feast was held which is still spoken of today. An envoy was sent to the Rajah of Bengal, informing him that the Princess was alive and well and married to her beloved Prince. In the passing of the months, the Rajah himself came to visit his daughter, seated upon an elephant and bearing gifts and blessings for the happy pair.

As for the flying horse, the wise Shah took out the cock's head pegs so that no one should use the horse again and meet with misfortune.

The Prince and the Princess rose up, up, up into the air and flew away.

65

Princess Budoor and Prince Camaralzaman

THERE WAS IN ANCIENT TIMES a king named Shah Zaman who ruled the Islands of Khalidan, just off the coast of Persia. Although the Shah had four young wives and a harem of sixty female slaves, he was growing old and had no son and heir. This distressed him so much that one day he summoned all his holy men to try their magic, hoping this might help.

Within a year his third wife gave birth to a son as handsome as the full moon in a starlit sky. He was named 'Moon of the Age' or Camar-al-Zaman. And the young Prince grew up in such love and tender care that he became a charming, clever youth.

One day, when the boy was fifteen, the Shah called Camaralzaman to him. 'My dear son,' he said, 'I am old and you will soon be King; my fondest wish is to see you wed before I die.'

But Prince Camaralzaman shook his head. 'O my Father,' he said sadly, 'I have no desire to marry; my heart has no place for women. And the books I have read warn me of their treachery and deceit. As the poet says:

> *If you ask my opinion of women,*
> *I will tell you,*
> *I know them well.*
> *When a man's head is grey*
> *And his wealth declines,*
> *Their love will turn to scorn.*

'I would rather drink a cup of poison than yield to a woman's wiles.'

When Shah Zaman heard these words, light turned to darkness before his eyes and he was sorely grieved by his son's disobedience. Yet he loved him so much that he could not be angry for long.

Meanwhile, the young Prince daily became more handsome and elegant. Each zephyr that wafted its gentle breeze sang of his praises: of his face that put the pale moon to shame; of his dark hair that was blacker than the darkest night; of his slender form that resembled a branch of an oriental willow or Indian cane.

One year later, the Shah summoned his son to him once again and repeated what he had said a year before: 'O my son, I am old and feeble and you will soon be King; my fondest wish is to see you wed before I die.'

But Camaralzaman refused, quoting the poet again:

With their fingers dyed with henna
And their hair arranged in plaits;
With their eyelids painted silver
And their honeyed lips sublime,
They trap unwary men
And make them forever drink
Their draught of sorrow.

When the Shah heard these words, he grew sad and silent. But he did not punish his son for his disobedience. He suffered another year, then called his son again and repeated as before, 'My only son, I will die soon; my dying wish is that you marry a lady of your choice, so that our realm will have a Queen.'

His son, however, was just as stubborn as before: he said he would never wed. This time the Shah flew into a rage and banished the Prince to the palace tower, telling him he would remain there until he changed his mind.

So the Prince found himself lying upon a mattress in a lofty tower, with no one for company except a eunuch guarding the door. How he cursed all women, marriage and the evil of the opposite sex. Only when his anger cooled did he cover himself with a silken sheet and sleep, unaware of the strange adventures that were about to overtake him.

Now, this room in the tower had been untenanted for many years; in the corner was a Roman well in which there dwelt a female genie named Maymoona, the daughter of Dimiriat, King of a noble tribe of genies. That night, as Maymoona floated up the well, she was surprised to find two candles burning in the tower, one at the head and one at the foot of a sleeping figure lying on a mattress. Being curious, she came closer and saw the Prince. She had never set eyes on such a handsome man in all her life – and she was now a thousand years old. So she bent down and kissed him on the brow.

With a sigh, she then continued her ascent into the sky until she reached the lower heavens. And here she met another genie flying through the air. It was Dahnash, the boyfriend of Maymoona (for love exists among the genies, too). And they set to recounting what they had seen and heard that night.

'Dear Maymoona,' said Dahnash, 'I come from the furthest part of China, from the land of a King with seven palaces. That monarch has a daughter, Princess Budoor – Ah, Allah has created no human more beautiful in the world; my tongue is too short to describe her loveliness. As she turns up her fair face towards the moon, the earth and sky share

two pale moons. She has cheeks like deep red wine, lips of coral and carnelian; the juices of her mouth are like melted honey, and her sparkling teeth are like a string of pearls. Her skin is as smooth as silk, and her tongue is moved only by cultured words.

'Her father loves her to distraction and had the seven palaces erected in her honour. As the fame of her beauty spread far and wide, many were the suitors who came to seek her hand. But she told her father: "I have no wish to marry. I am a Princess, a future Queen who will one day rule men. I need no man to rule over me. In any case, men are all vain and cruel, never content to love a single wife. As the poet says:

> Beware of men,
> For they will force you to obey.
> The maid will not prosper
> Who surrenders to them;
> They will stop her from learning
> Of science and life,
> For most of all they fear
> The liberation of her mind."

'When her father heard these words he was so angry that he confined her to an upstairs room, with ten senior women, her karamanes, to guard her day and night.'

The genie finished his story to Maymoona by confessing that every night he gazed upon the lovely Princess and gently kissed her brow while she was asleep. 'Such is her beauty; no one can match her in the world,' he sighed.

The genie Maymoona smiled. 'But you are wrong,' she said. And she began to relate her own adventures of the night just passed.

'Beside a Prince I know, your so-called beauty is but a faded rose. My Prince is flawless, a pearl among pebbles on the shore, a ruby in a bowl of marbles, an emerald amid dried peas, a sapphire mingled with ambergris . . .'

So she went on citing all the precious stones; this only irritated her companion, who claimed that he was right. Thus they quarrelled, each certain of the truth and more than a trifle jealous. In the end it was agreed that Dahnash would bring his Princess and lay her down beside the Prince, the better to judge who was more beautiful.

Off flew Dahnash to the furthest part of China and soon returned carrying the sleeping maid. When the Prince and Princess lay side by side in sweet repose, the two genies resumed their dispute.

'My Princess is more lovely than your Prince!'

'Fiddlesticks! My Prince is more handsome than your Princess!'

Neither would concede.

So finally they agreed to seek a third opinion. As Maymoona stamped upon the floor, an old, old genie appeared: it was Coosh-Coosh, the wise sage. On learning of the disagreement, he looked down

Coosh-Coosh looked down upon the sleeping pair and wondered at their beauty.

upon the sleeping pair and wondered at their beauty. After some time he sighed and quietly said, 'By Allah, they are so alike in beauty and perfection that I cannot choose between them. Perhaps we might try another way of settling the argument: let us wake them both in turn and see which one falls more deeply in love with the other; that one will be the loser.'

It was agreed.

Thereupon, Maymoona turned herself into a flea and bit the Prince upon his neck; this made him scratch and move. As he did so he felt someone lying by his side, with breath more fragrant than musk and a body softer than butter. All sleep deserted him at once. Raising himself on one arm he gazed in surprise at the damsel beside him. He touched

69

her gently, but she slept on – for Dahnash had put her into a heavy slumber.

Then the Prince took her hand and pressed it; but she would not wake. For a long hour he gazed fondly upon her, falling more and more in love as each minute passed.

'My father must have put her here to test me,' he said to himself. 'Well, his wish is fulfilled, for I would gladly spend my life with her, she is so beautiful.'

With that he bent over the sleeping Princess Budoor and went to kiss her lips. As he did so, Dahnash let out a cry of joy, while Maymoona trembled with dismay – for the other genie, it seemed, had won.

But just as Prince Camaralzaman was about to plant a kiss, he suddenly turned away. It was not right to steal a kiss without permission; instead, he took the ring off his middle finger and slipped it on her own, as a token of his love. Then he lay back and was soon asleep.

Now it was Maymoona's turn to celebrate. 'Did you see how my Prince looked at, yet did not kiss, your beauty?

He gazed fondly upon her, falling more and more in love as each minute passed.

Instead he turned his back and slept.'

The crestfallen Dahnash said nothing. Then, turning himself into a flea, he bit the sleeping Princess Budoor on the neck, at which she opened her eyes in irritation. All at once she sat up in alarm as she saw the young man beside her, softly snoring in his sleep. She let out a stifled scream.

'Oh disgrace!' she cried. 'A stranger in my bed, lying here beside me!'

Then, stealing a glance at him again, her fears slowly dissolved into love. 'By Allah,' she sighed, 'my heart is pierced by the sword of passion as I gaze on his handsome form. Such love is no disgrace. If this is the man my father wishes me to wed, I will do so willingly. No doubt the King has put this young man here to test me.'

With that she took the Prince's hand to wake him. But the genie's enchantment caused him to slumber on, so that no words or shaking could arouse him. Camaralzaman snored on contentedly in his sleep. All at once the Princess noticed a strange ring upon her middle finger. How did that get there, she wondered? And as a token of her love she took her own ring from the middle finger of her other hand and slipped it upon his little finger. With a sigh, she tenderly kissed his hand and, placing her arm about his neck, she fell asleep again beside him.

That settled it. The genie Maymoona was content: she thanked wise old Coosh-Coosh, and sent off the dejected Dahnash with the lovely Princess back to her land. When that was done the genies left the royal pair to sleep through the night in their own beds, far distant from each other.

When daybreak came, Camaralzaman awoke from his sleep and looked round for the lovely maid. But no one was there. Could it all have been a dream? Summoning the eunuch guard, he asked him about the beautiful maid who had shared his mattress in the night.

'Master,' the eunuch said, 'how could a maid pass by me in the night when I was wide awake?'

Fearing that the Prince was going mad, the eunuch reported to the Shah, who went to see his son forthwith. As soon as the old king appeared, his son met him with a smile and his happy news.

'I agree to marry, Father,' he said at once, 'on condition that you wed me to the maid who lay beside me in the night. Obviously you sent her here to test me.'

And he related to his father all that had transpired in the night, even showing him the maiden's ring upon his finger. But the Shah confessed he knew nothing of the girl.

'For the love of Allah,' cried the Prince at last, 'find that maid and fetch her here, or I shall die of grief.'

The poor Shah, full of remorse for banishing his son, had him put in a sickroom overlooking the sea. Yet as the days wore on, the young man

pined away, hardly taking food or drink. All the while the old Shah sat by his bed, mourning and weeping for his son, never leaving him night or day.

In the meantime, thousands of miles away in the furthest part of China, Princess Budoor had woken in her bed and glanced about her in despair. For the handsome youth was gone. At her sharp cry, all her nursemaids, the ten old karamanes, came in to see what ailed her.

'Where is the man who lay in my arms this night just past ?' she cried. 'What have you done with him ? Bring him here at once or I shall die of grief!'

The nursemaids tried to calm her down, assuring her that no man had passed them in the night. But, remembering the ring, Princess Budoor held up her hand for all to see.

'Look at this,' she cried triumphantly, 'here is his ring!'

The nursemaids all felt pity for the poor Princess, certain she had lost her reason. And the King was called.

'What is it that ails you, daughter?' he asked.

'Where is the young man who slept beside me in the night?' she cried pitifully.

And when no one could answer her, she really did lose her senses, tearing out her hair and rending her clothes to tatters. So violent was her fury that the King feared for her life and had her bound by an iron chain fixed from her neck to the window bars.

Thus she was prevented from harming herself while her father sought a cure. He summoned sages and astrologers from all over China, solemnly proclaiming, 'Any man that cures my daughter may marry her and take half of my kingdom. But if he should fail, his head will be cut off and stuck upon the palace gate.'

*So violent was her fury
that the King had her bound
by an iron chain fixed from
her neck to the window bars.*

There were plenty of men who came to try and cure her. But none succeeded. And soon the palace gate was stuck with more than forty heads. The Shah consulted all his court magicians and even men of science. But no cure was found.

Three years went by. The lady Budoor did not recover. Indeed, she was almost on the point of death.

Now, the Princess had a cousin named Marzawan who had been travelling abroad these past three years; on returning home he heard of her sad history for the first time. Gaining entry to her chamber by bribing the eunuch guard, he listened patiently to her story. She concluded by telling him, 'They say that I am mad, that I rave of whom I love. And I reply: the sweetest fruits of life are only for the insane. Bring me the one I love and I will straightaway be cured.'

Marzawan could see she really was suffering from the deepest love (for, truth to tell, he had suffered thus himself from his love for Princess Budoor; it was because she refused him that he had travelled about the world these past three years to mend his soul).

'I will go in search of the object of your love, dear Princess,' her cousin said. 'Allah be willing, I shall return soon with news. Pray be patient.'

Marzawan set off on his mission, wandering from town to town, island to island, land to land. And everywhere folk had heard of the madness of the lovely Princess, but no one knew of its cause. Then, after a month, he came to the port of Et-Tereb; and here he heard the tale of a Persian Prince who was afflicted no less strongly than his cousin, seemingly of the same disease.

At once he set sail for the Islands of Khalidan off the coast of Persia, and in three weeks arrived at the Shah's palace where the dying prince lay. On informing the guards that he was an astrologer from China come to cure the Prince, he was conducted to the Shah and told the entire story.

'Three years ago,' the Shah began, 'I asked my son to wed, and when he refused I shut him in a tower. Next morning he awoke and claimed he had been sleeping beside a maiden of surpassing beauty. He even showed me her ring. Of course, it was all a dream; the poor boy is mad.'

When he had heard the story, Marzawan felt sure he had at last found the key to unlock his cousin's mind. For the moment, however, he kept the secret to himself; he only asked to see the Prince. On entering the sickroom that overlooked the sea, he saw the Prince stretched out upon his bed, pale as death, his eyes closed in resignation. Marzawan waved away his escort and sat down beside the Prince's bed.

'Strengthen your heart,' he said. 'Your Princess also pines for you; but she is chained by the neck to her prison bars. Her name is Princess Budoor and I shall take you to her just as soon as you are well.'

And just to prove that what he said was true, Marzawan showed the

The two men set off on the long journey to China.

Prince the ring which he had given to Budoor as a token of his love. The envoy continued to encourage the Prince until his appetite returned and he recovered from his illness.

One day, when the Prince was completely well, he told the envoy, 'Now is the time for you to keep your vow: take me to my beloved Princess. But there is one more obstacle to overcome: my father is so concerned about me he will not let me out of his sight.'

'Fear not,' said Marzawan. 'Go to your father and say you are leaving on a hunting trip with me; let him have a pair of good horses ready for us at dawn.'

Thinking the fresh air and sun would be beneficial to the Prince, the Shah gave his consent and, next day at dawn, the two men set off to make the long journey to the furthest part of China. After many weeks they finally came to that part of China where the Princess Budoor lived. As they rode into the city, Marzawan gave the Prince instructions on how to gain admittance to the mad Princess, and he had him equipped as an astrologer.

Next morning, Camaralzaman went forth to the palace, holding a

*'I come to cure the Princess Budoor
and win her hand.'*

set of geometric instruments and dressed for his part. He stood before
the palace gates staring up at the rotting heads impaled upon the spikes,
and shouted out, 'I am an astrologer and a scribe. I come to cure the
Princess Budoor and win her hand.'

The townsfolk quickly crowded round. It was several months since
anyone had risked his neck, and all the Chinese astrologers were now
dead. Seeing the handsome youth, they urged him to set aside his
ambition. However, instead of listening to their pleas, he cried even
more loudly than before, 'I am an astrologer and a scribe. I come to cure
the Princess Budoor and win her hand.'

While he was shouting thus, the King sent out his Vizier to let in the
foolish man; but when the King set eyes upon the young and handsome
Prince he was truly sorry that he might have to die.

'Young man,' he said, 'though I treasure my daughter's health, I do
not wish you to die. Call off your mission.'

But Camaralzaman would not be swayed. At last he was conducted
by a eunuch to Princess Budoor's chamber. He was in such a hurry to
see her that the eunuch could not keep up.

76

'Hold on, friend,' he cried. 'By Allah, I never knew an astrologer so eager to meet his doom. You are bound to lose your head, so why not savour your last moments more slowly?'

'You evidently doubt my powers,' said the Prince with a smile. 'And what if I tell you I can cure your mistress without even seeing her? Just seat me behind the curtain to her room and let me write the Princess a note.'

So the eunuch sat him down behind the curtain and watched with curiosity as he took out his writing case and began a letter.

> My Dear Princess,
>   I write with a heart overflowing with love for you, with eyes weary from shedding many tears, with a body wasted from longing and grief. I am a restless wanderer whose eye never sleeps, the slave of love whose tears never cease, the victim of fate whose flame of desire never dies.
>   Once I awoke to behold a maiden in my bed and exchanged my ring with hers. Here is the token of my eternal love.
>
>   Prince Camaralzaman

As he sealed the letter he carefully enclosed the ring, handing it to the eunuch who took it to the Princess.

As soon as she had read the note and found the ring, she knew that her beloved Prince had come at last. And now all reason did fly from her as joy multiplied her strength. Pressing her feet against the wall, she strained with all her might and broke the iron collar from her neck, together with the chains. Then she rushed to her beloved and took him in her arms. They kissed and wept, so happy were they to be together once again.

Meanwhile, at a call from the eunuch, the King came at once and rejoiced to see his daughter cured. Placing the Princess Budoor's hand in that of the handsome stranger, he said gravely, 'I keep my promise and give you my daughter as your wife.'

Thereupon, Prince Camaralzaman told the King all about himself and the amazing adventures that had led to his everlasting love.

'Such a wonderful tale of love must be written down and recorded in books,' said the King, 'so that all may read it, from one age to the next.'

A wedding banquet was prepared, the city was garlanded for seven days and never was such a happy couple seen in all the world. The faithful Marzawan was not forgotten: he was granted a high post at court for bringing the pair together. And shortly after, the Prince and Princess set out to the Islands of Khalidan to greet the Shah, who was no less delighted than the Chinese King.

And in the passing of the years, the wise Queen Budoor and King Camaralzaman ruled together over both China and Persia.

Gulnara, the Brave and Clever Maiden

HERE WAS ONCE AN EMPEROR OF PERSIA named Shah Khunoo. He often wandered in disguise about his city attended by the Grand Vizier, and he met with many strange adventures.

On one occasion, as the Shah was walking through a narrow street in the poor part of the capital, he heard some voices coming from a house. Being curious, he put his eye to the window and saw three sisters sitting on a sofa chatting together. By what the eldest said, he understood them to be talking of whom they wished to wed.

'If I had a wish,' said the eldest girl, 'I would marry the Shah's chief baker, then I should have all the bread and cakes I fancied.'

'If I had my wish,' said the second girl, 'I would wed the Shah's chief cook, then I should have all the dishes I desired.'

The youngest sister, the cleverest of the three who was also bold and skilful, spoke up next: 'Since it is only a wish that will not come true, I would marry the Shah himself. I would bear him a handsome son whose hair would be gold on one side and silver on the other; and when he cried the tears from his eyes would be as pearls; and when he smiled, his lips would be as a parting rose-bud.'

The three wishes amused the Shah and he resolved that they should be fulfilled. On his return to the palace he therefore instructed his Vizier to bring the sisters to him on the following day. Thus it was: the three trembling girls stood before the Shah on the morrow.

'Do you recall the wishes you made last night?' he asked them.

At these unexpected words, the girls all blushed the deepest scarlet and cast down their eyes in modesty and shame. Seeing them so confused, the Shah smiled and said, 'I did not mean to distress you; indeed, I know your wishes and intend to make them come true. You who wished to wed my baker shall do so today; and you who wished to wed my cook shall do so tomorrow. And as for you, young lady, who wished to be my wife, well you shall have your wish the day after that.'

And so in the next three days three marriages were celebrated, each according to the husband's rank. Of course, the wedding of the Shah

78

'Do you recall the wishes you made
last night?' he asked them.

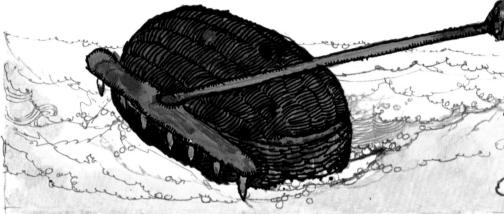

*The Shah's gardener drew the basket
to the bank with a rake.*

and his young bride was the most magnificent by far, and it caused the other sisters much envy. How they now wished they had chosen the Shah themselves!

Thereafter the two sisters often came together to gossip and plot revenge upon the Queen.

Within the year the Queen gave birth to a young prince as handsome and bright as the morning sun. But the two sisters, who attended the Queen at birth, wrapped him up and put him in a basket which they threw into the river by the palace. And they told the Shah that his and their sister's baby had been stillborn. This made him very sad.

Meanwhile, the basket with the baby prince drifted past the garden of the Shah's head gardener. Seeing the basket, he drew it to the bank with a rake and was amazed to find an infant inside. Since Allah had never blessed him and his wife with a child, he took the baby home to his delighted wife and they brought it up as their own.

The following year the Queen gave birth again, this time to twins, a girl and a boy. The wicked sisters cruelly pretended these children had been stillborn, too; and they sent them down the river as before. By good fortune, the basket containing the twins was found by the head gardener again, and the infants were taken home to his wife.

80

Shah Khunoo could not disguise his disappointment, and had his wife banished to a hut beside the mosque, so that she might be spat upon by his subjects as they went to prayer. She bore her unjust punishment with such fortitude that she soon earned the admiration of all who had compassion.

In the meantime the two princes and the princess were nursed by the gardener and his wife with all the tender care of two devoted parents. They named the two princes Bahman and Perviz, and the princess Gulnara. As soon as the children were old enough, the gardener employed a master to teach them how to read and write, to sing and to play musical instruments. Gulnara by her wit and nimble hands soon excelled above her brothers. And when the brothers learned to ride and shoot an arrow, she joined in and soon excelled at those sports too; she could even beat them in running races, jumping, wrestling and throwing the spear.

Now the gardener and his wife were growing old and decided to retire to the country. However, after they and their family had lived at their new country home for six months, illness came and carried off the old pair. So sudden were their deaths that neither had time to tell the children the tale of their discovery. And so the three children grew up

with only themselves for company, free from the false ambitions of those at court. They led happy, contented, simple lives and loved each other dearly.

One day, while the two brothers were out hunting and Gulnara was at home, a wandering holy woman chanced to call; she wished to borrow a prayer mat on which to say her prayers. Gulnara warmly welcomed her, showed her into the little room that served as their chapel and prepared her a meal.

'Since you have been so kind,' the wayfarer said on parting, 'I wish to tell you of three wonders that can be yours. The first is a speaking bird which, when it lifts up its voice to sing, is accompanied in chorus by all the songbirds of the forest. The second is a singing tree whose leaves represent the seasons; each month forms a choir to sing that season's music. And the third is golden water which, when just one drop is poured into a bowl, fills up by itself, yet never overflows.'

'What an incredible story,' said the girl. 'But where, pray, are they to be found?'

'All are in a single place, some twenty days from here along the road to India,' the woman answered.

With that she took up her tiny bundle and went on her way. When her brothers returned, Gulnara told them of the woman and her tale, and they could see their sister was sad, longing to have these wonders.

'Cheer up, Gulnara,' said Bahman. 'Since you desire the speaking bird, the singing tree and the golden water, I shall fetch them for you. I commend you to my brother's care while I'm away.'

Next morning, Bahman mounted his horse and, before starting on his way, handed his sister a dagger in its sheath.

'Who knows what dangers I may encounter?' he said. 'To learn of my safety consult this dagger: if on taking it from its sheath the blade is clean, then I am safe; but if the blade is stained with blood, it is a sign that I am dead.'

Thereupon he spurred on his horse and went galloping away. On and on he rode, not turning to left or right, and as the twentieth day dawned he came upon an odd old man sitting at the roadside. His eyebrows were as white as snow, as was his beard which hung down to his feet; the nails on his hands and toes were two spans long, and he was naked save for a sack about his loins. He was evidently a dervish or a hermit, devoted to prayer and meditation.

'May Allah prolong your days, good father,' said Bahman in greeting. 'I would like to ask instructions from you.'

And he told the old man of his quest.

'Sir,' the old fellow mumbled into his beard, 'I know the way, but the dangers are greater than you suppose. A number of young men have passed by on that same quest, but none have returned. Turn back your horse, that is my advice.'

Nothing the hermit could say would deter Bahman. And in the end he put his hand into a bag and took out a bowl, which he handed to the young man.

'Since you ignore my warning, take this bowl, cast it before you and follow wherever it rolls, right to the foot of a tall mountain. There the bowl will stop. Dismount from your horse and climb the mountain; on your way you will see hundreds of big black rocks and hear a chorus of voices flinging insults at you. Be not afraid and, above all, do not glance back. For if you do, you will be turned that instant into blackest rock – the rocks all around you are young men who failed in their test. If you overcome those dangers and reach the mountain top you will find a cage; within it is the speaking bird. The bird will tell you how to find the singing tree and the golden water. That is all. Peace be with you.'

'And with you, old man,' said the lad.

He cast the bowl before him and followed it at a gallop until it halted at the foot of a tall mountain. All was just as the dervish had said: black rocks littered the mountainside and jeering voices muttered dark threats, making such a din the young man had to close his ears. One voice called, 'Where is he going?'

Others cried, 'Do not let him pass!' 'Stop him!' 'Kill him!' 'Knock him down!'

Yet others roared out like thunder, 'Thief!' 'Assassin!' 'Murderer!'

Despite the hubbub, Bahman boldly continued his ascent; but the voices created such a noise in front, behind and from all sides that his courage began to ebb away, his legs to tremble and his heart to fail. And, forgetting the dervish's advice, he turned about to run back down the slope. In an instant he was turned to stone.

In the meantime, Gulnara was keeping her brother's dagger in a girdle at her waist and pulled it out several times a day for a sign of her brother's safety. All went well until that fatal moment when he was turned to rock. As she drew the dagger from its sheath she was horrified to see blood running down the blade. How she cried with grief and remorse.

'Why did I have to tell him of those three enchanted things?' she wailed.

'Do not blame yourself,' Perviz said. 'It is Allah's will, so we must submit to it. But I must learn the truth about our brother; tomorrow I shall set out.'

Gulnara did all she could to change his mind, but without success. Before leaving, he handed her a string of a hundred pearls, saying, 'If, when you count them, dearest sister, they do not run freely along the string, that means I am in mortal danger.'

Despite her pleas to stay, he rode off next morning at dawn and, on the twentieth day, came to the same old dervish sitting by the wayside.

It was then he received news of his brother and the same warnings as before.

'Your brother has been turned to stone,' explained the dervish sadly. 'And so, too, will you be unless you obey my instructions.'

And the dervish repeated the speech he had made to Bahman, finally handing him a wooden bowl.

Casting the bowl before him. Perviz galloped off, arriving shortly at the foot of the mountain. When he had tied up his horse and climbed six paces up the slope, he heard a voice behind, jeering at him, 'Stop, thief, or face the fate of your cowardly brother!'

Upon this insult to his brother's name, he swung round, hand on sword; but no one was there. Immediately he was turned to stone.

She charged along the road like the wind.

Back home in their cottage, his sister was all the while fearfully counting the hundred beads; even at night she woke up to count them several times. But now, the moment he was turned to stone, she could not roll the pearls along the string – and she knew that he was dead.

She did not cry or grieve. Instead she set out at once to learn of her brothers' fate. Girding on her sword and dagger, she mounted a horse and charged like the wind along the road to India. Twenty days later she halted at the dervish and received the same instructions as her brothers. Following the bowl, she arrived at length at the mountain foot; there she dismounted and, unlike her brothers, she blocked her ears with cloth.

And she began to climb. Dimly she heard mutterings all about her as she clambered bravely towards the top. The higher she went, the louder the voices were, and she could now hear quite distinctly their insulting words. But she laughed out loud and did not turn her head.

Finally she reached the top, and there she found the speaking bird. As she set her hand upon the cage, the chorus of voices stopped and she took the cloth from her ears.

'Brave girl,' the bird said to her, 'I am yours to do with as you wish. I know who you are, for you are not what you think yourself; one day I shall tell you more. For the moment, do as I say. Fill this little silver flask inside my cage with golden water from the stream nearby and take a branch from that tree alongside the water; plant it at home and it will grow into the singing tree.'

Gulnara did as she was bid, then asked, 'Bird, how may I save my brothers from their fate?'

'Sprinkle a little of the water from your flask,' it said, 'upon each rock along the mountain path and that will break the spell.'

On her way down she gave life to a hundred men, including her two brothers. Riding at the head of the grateful band, Gulnara led them back along the road from India. One by one they left her as they returned to their own lands, but not before they had thanked her warmly for saving their lives.

As soon as Gulnara and her brothers reached home, she placed the cage upon a stand in the garden, and the bird began to sing. In no time at all it was surrounded by larks and linnets, goldfinches, chaffinches, nightingales and swallows, every type of bird in the land. How beautifully they all sang.

In the centre of the garden she planted the branch of the singing tree and, in three days, it had grown into a stately tree, its leaves murmuring in the breeze so sweetly that it blended perfectly with the season's mood.

She placed a marble bowl in the garden and emptied into it the contents of her flask; the golden water at once swelled up and formed a fountain spouting to the sky, yet never spilling from the bowl.

News of these wonders soon spread throughout the land and, since the gates of the house and garden were never closed, visitors came from far and wide to see them.

Among those to hear of the enchanting music and the golden fountain was the Shah, who decided to see the wonders for himself. So one day he came to the cottage and announced himself, explaining the reason for his visit.

Of course, the two brothers were greatly honoured and not a little awed. But Gulnara showed no fear of the mighty monarch, and gladly showed him round her garden.

'My good maid,' said the Shah, 'where are all the musicians that I hear? Such splendid performers would lose nothing by being in view.'

'Sire,' Gulnara said, 'they are but the leaves of this tree which you see before you rustling in the breeze.'

Then, gazing up at the golden fountain, the Shah exclaimed in wonder, 'But where is its source? I see no stream or force to make it leap so high. Truly, I have never seen the like in all my years.'

Gulnara patiently explained how the fountain had come from just a tiny flask and that no stream was connected to it.

Glancing round the garden, the Shah next marvelled at the singing of the many colourful birds around.

'What brings so many birds here?' he asked. 'Even my palace gardens do not possess such a variety of birds and song.'

'The reason is my speaking bird,' she said. 'All the birds of the world come from far and near to accompany its song.'

And, turning to the bird, the young maid said, 'Bird, here is Shah Khunoo, come to pay his compliments to you.'

The bird stopped singing at once, silencing the birdsong chorus. 'Long live the Shah,' it said.

The astonished emperor stared at the bird in even greater surprise, saying, 'Sultan of all the birds, I thank you for your song. These wonders fill me with amazement.'

'Can you be surprised by what you see when you are deceived by what you hear?' the bird spoke up.

The Shah asked the meaning of these words, at which the bird sternly replied, 'Why did you believe so readily that your Queen had given birth to three stillborn babies?'

The Shah was so surprised that he did not take offence; instead he rejoined, 'But the Queen's own sisters assured me it was so.'

'Those sisters, sire,' said the bird, 'were jealous of the Queen and deceived you to gain revenge. If you press them now they will confess to their crime. The two brothers and sister you see before you are, in truth, your own children; they were rescued by your gardener and brought up as his own.'

The Shah was just as astonished as Gulnara and her brothers. But the truth of what the bird had said touched his heart at once – for the three young people were so like the Queen. In tears he embraced his children, begging their forgiveness for the lost years.

'It is not for us to pardon you,' Gulnara said. 'It is our mother, if she is still alive.'

In haste, the Shah mounted his horse, asking his children to follow within three days, and he rushed off towards the town, tears streaming behind him in the wind.

When he arrived at the hut beside the mosque, he opened the door in great remorse and fell to his knees before the Queen, begging pardon for all the harm he had done. Although she was ill and in rags, the noble woman forgave him for the long years of insult and misery she had suffered. 'You were deceived by my own sisters,' she said. 'It was not your fault. Allah be praised that we have found our dear children; now let us forget the past and make the most of our remaining years.'

Taking his wife back to the palace, he tended to her more lovingly than any husband ever has to any wife. And at once, despite his wife's protestations, he had the two evil sisters put to death.

At the end of three days and nights, the Princess Gulnara led her brothers to the city and into the royal palace. They were cheered all through the streets by townsfolk rejoicing at the news; and every house and street was garlanded with flowers to mark their safe return. With them came the bird in its golden cage, accompanied by a flock of singing birds; henceforth, the rooftops of the city were to ring to the most enchanting birdsong.

Of course, upon the family's reunion the tears flowed freely down the cheeks of all, especially the Queen, so happy was she to see her children after so many years.

Such were the celebrations that they are still talked of to this day in the quiet of a Persian evening.

Ali Baba and the Forty Thieves

ONG, LONG AGO IN A PERSIAN CITY, there once lived two brothers: Cassim and Ali Baba. Cassim married a wealthy woman, and in no time at all became a well-to-do merchant with a shop and a mansion. Ali, however, wed a woman as poor as she was honest, and lived by woodcutting; he sold his logs for firewood at the bazaar.

One day, when Ali Baba was in the forest with his donkey, cutting wood, he was surprised to hear the thud-thud-thud of hoofs coming along the forest path. As quickly as he could he hid his donkey and clambered up a tree standing beside a rocky slope.

To his dismay, the men rode right up to the tree in which he was hiding. Ali counted forty of them, and from their looks they were either thieves or bandits. When they had dismounted from their horses and were busy unloading their saddlebags, their leader stood before a large rock and shouted, 'Open sesame!'

'Open sesame!'

No sooner had he spoken than the rocky wall began to move and a doorway appeared, wide enough for the men to pass through one by one. It then closed behind them just as neatly as if it had never been. As Ali watched, afraid of being discovered, the men emerged from the cave a few minutes later, remounted their steeds and rode away – but not before the bandit chief had cried, 'Shut sesame!'

And the rock door swung closed.

When the hoofbeats had died away, Ali swiftly scrambled down his tree and went up to the rocky wall. Examining it carefully, he was surprised to find no crack or split anywhere at all. Remembering the chieftain's words, he then said in a trembling voice, 'Open sesame!'

To his astonishment, the rockface opened up. Ali stood staring into the dark beyond, then, plucking up courage, he passed inside; he had not gone more than three steps when the door swung shut behind him. But before he could worry about escape he suddenly caught sight of the

cave's contents. The place was piled high with treasure of every sort: rich bales of silk, brocade and costly carpets, sacks of gold and silver coin, pearls and rubies, glittering bracelets and necklaces – all spilling out from their chests and sacks over the floor.

Now, Ali was not a greedy man. He helped himself to no more than a small sackful of golden coin, just enough for his donkey to bear, and stood before the doorway once again. Saying the magic words, he passed through into the bright daylight and loaded up his mount. Once more, he turned back to the cave, uttered the words 'Shut sesame' and, as the rock took on its normal form, he went home with his donkey.

Once home, he showed his wife the gold and told her the whole astounding story.

'Morgiana,' Ali said to his wife, 'we had best bury the gold lest it be found and we are thought to be the thieves.'

'Let me weigh it first,' she said, 'so that we know how much there is. Wait, I'll borrow some scales from your brother Cassim, while you are digging a hole in the yard.'

Off she ran for the scales, not letting Cassim's wife into the secret. But the woman, being a busybody, rubbed some sticky suet on the underside of the scales, so that whatever was being weighed would likely stick to it.

Her ruse worked well and when the scales were returned, Cassim's wife was surprised to find a shining piece of gold sticking to the bottom of the scales. That made her exceedingly jealous; at once she showed the gold coin to her husband and neither of them slept a wink that night. First thing the next day Cassim went to his brother to learn the secret of his new-found fortune.

'If you don't own up,' yelled the envious man, 'I'll report you to the judge and he will try you as a thief.'

So Ali Baba told his story.

Hastening home, the greedy Cassim broke the news to his wife and, together, they quickly loaded ten asses with large sacks; then he set off for the hillside rock that Ali had described. As soon as he arrived, he scrambled from his ass, crying at the top of his voice, 'Open sesame!'

And at once the cave door opened, inviting him inside, then closed again. His eyes popping at the sparkling treasure about his feet, Cassim eagerly filled his sacks and hauled each in turn to the cave doorway, ready to carry out.

But in his excitement, poor Cassim let the password slip clean from his mind. All he remembered was that it was connected with some seed or grain.

'Open rice!' . . . 'Open caraway!' . . . 'Open rye!' . . . 'Open barley!'

'Open all sorts of seed and grain!' he cried in a frenzy.

To no avail. The more desperate he became, the more fuddled was his brain; frantically he tried to escape by any means, yet he could not.

*His eyes popped at
the sparkling treasure
about his feet.*

He was a prisoner in the cave.

About noon, the robber band returned. On seeing the group of asses tethered there, the forty thieves leapt from their horses, intent on slaying whoever had learned their secret.

Poor Cassim. He could hear the angry muttering, the clang and clash of swords, and then – oh Allah the all-merciful – the voice of the chieftain shouting out the words he recalled too late: 'Open sesame!'

The rock door slowly opened. Knowing he was doomed, Cassim made a dash for it, knocked down the robber chief, but was then cut to ribbons by the other thieves. The robbers hung each of his limbs inside the doorway – as a warning to whoever else might enter their cave.

Thereupon, off they rode in search of more caravans and innocent wayfarers to rob.

Throughout the day Cassim's wife waited for her husband to come home, happy at the thought of the riches he would bring. But as night drew on, her joy turned to fear, and she ran to Ali Baba's for advice – of course, she had to tell him where Cassim had gone.

In the middle of the night, Ali stole into the forest and made for the cave; and when he entered, torch in hand, he was horrified to find the pieces of his brother's body, blood still dripping to the cave's stone floor. He gathered up all the remains, wrapped them in sacking and loaded them along with the sacks of treasure on to Cassim's asses before returning home.

'What am I to do with Cassim's body?' he asked his wife. 'If his widow sees the poor man in this state she may confess everything to the judge and we'll all be destined for an early grave.'

Morgiana was wise as well as brave. 'Leave it to me,' was all she said.

At dawn next day, she went to the bazaar and sought out an old cobbler, Baba Mustafa by name. Giving him a golden coin she led him home and showed him Cassim's body in the sacking.

'I want you to stitch the pieces together to make him as good as new,' she said. 'Do your task well and I shall reward you with more money than you earn in a year.'

Baba Mustafa set to work as if stitching a giant pair of shoes. And such was his skill that he soon had all the pieces back in place with hardly a sign of seams.

Only then was Cassim's wife told the news and allowed to view her husband's remains. The funeral passed off without a fuss: neither the Imam at the mosque, nor any of the mourners could guess what had happened to the body. Baba Mustafa was sworn to silence and rewarded well. Everything possible was done to hush up the affair.

In the meantime, the forty thieves visited their cave and found the body gone. It was then they realized that someone else knew of their secret and, therefore, had to be slain. But first this person had to be found.

'One of you must go to the city,' snarled the robber chief, 'and find out news of a body that has been hacked to pieces and only recently interred.'

So it was that next day at dawn one of the forty thieves, a crafty wily fellow, was wandering through the bazaar in the city, listening to gossip. His enquiries brought him at last to Baba Mustafa, busy stitching some sandals.

'Tell me, cobbler,' said the thief, 'your trade must tire your aged eyes and hands.'

Glancing up from his work, the cobbler proudly replied, 'Old as I am, my eyes and fingers never fail me. Why, do you know, the other day I stitched together the bits and pieces of a body that had been hacked apart.'

'A body?' exclaimed the thief, pretending to be surprised. 'Where, pray, was that?'

'I was led to a house down by the river and paid well for my skill,' the cobbler said.

'If you take me there I'll give you double what you earned,' the robber promised.

So saying, he put ten gold pieces in the cobbler's hand and followed him through the winding streets, down towards the river until they stopped at the gates of Ali Baba's house. Having paid off his informant, the thief took a piece of chalk and drew a white cross upon the gates; then he hurried back to the bandits' cave to tell his news.

By and by, Morgiana was going out to do her shopping and, as she returned, noticed the chalk cross on the gate. 'Whatever is its meaning?' she mused. 'It can only omen mischief.'

So, fetching a piece of white chalk, the clever woman made a cross on a dozen other gates without being seen. She did not mention the strange sign to her husband.

Before dawn next day, the forty thieves with the wily guide at their head came creeping into the city and made for Ali Baba's street. But what was this?

Not one, but a dozen houses in the street were marked with chalk.

Despite the man's protestations that he had marked a single gate, the bandit chief had him marched back to the cave and his head cut off. Then he despatched another thief to town, with strict orders not to fail, or he would share the fate of his headless companion. The second scout found Baba Mustafa, went to Ali Baba's house and this time marked the gate with a tiny cross in red chalk that only the keenest eye could spot.

But Morgiana had sharp eyes as well as wits and the red cross did not escape her gaze. She fetched a piece of red chalk and marked likewise all the houses in the street, so that when the robber band crept into town next day at dawn they were foiled yet again.

And another brigand's black-bearded head rolled across the ground

'Peace be with you, sir,' he said to Ali.

beside the cave to pay for his failure.

Having lost two men from his band, the chieftain decided this time to do the job himself. Accordingly, he bribed Baba Mustafa, and was taken to Ali Baba's house. The chief made no mark upon the gate: instead, he stared hard at the house, storing the picture in his memory.

On the way back to his men he thought up a clever plan. The thieves were to purchase thirty-seven empty jars in the bazaar, large enough for a man to hide inside; and they were to buy one more, filled with oil.

When all this was done, the chieftain, in the guise of a merchant of oil, set out from the cave with a pack of mules, each one loaded with two jars. And in each jar, except that filled with oil, was one of the thirty-seven thieves. The chieftain led his pack of mules through the town until he came at sunset to Ali Baba's door. And there he knocked politely.

'Peace be with you, sir,' he said to Ali. 'I am a stranger in your city, bound for tomorrow's market. Since I have nowhere to spend the night and tie up my mules, I wonder whether you, O gracious master, would show me kindness, for the love of Allah?'

Ali did not recognize the robber chief in his disguise and readily welcomed the traveller to spend the night with him; he opened the gates of his courtyard for the mules to enter with their thirty-eight jars of what he supposed was oil. Morgiana prepared a tasty supper for the guest and the evening passed in friendly conversation. At last, as it was getting late, the guest excused himself, saying he had to see to the mules for the night before retiring to his bed.

In truth, the chieftain went into the yard to give instructions to his men. 'I'll throw stones from my window – that's the signal.'

He whispered the message hoarsely to each of the thirty-seven men in the jars; then he went to his room to wait until the household was asleep.

In the meantime, Ali Baba went to bed and Morgiana remained alone, clearing away the bowls and remnants of the meal. Suddenly the kitchen lamp went out.

'Oh dear, it has run out of oil,' Morgiana sighed. 'And I've no oil in the house.'

Then she remembered all the oil jars standing in her yard. Thinking their guest wouldn't mind giving her enough oil for the lamp, she took a ladle and went to help herself. Just as she went to lift the lid from the first jar, her ladle banged against its side and she got a dreadful shock: a man's sharp voice came from within the jar: 'Is that the signal, chief?'

Though naturally scared at discovering that a man was inside the jar instead of oil, she quickly realized that she and Ali were in great danger. Disguising her voice, she said in low hoarse tones, 'Not yet. Not yet.'

Then stealthily she crept to all the other jars, tapping her ladle on the side and answering to their queries, 'Not yet. Not yet.'

Finally, she came to the jar of oil and helped herself to all of it. Using several pails to carry it into the house, she relit the lamp and put the rest of the oil in a big pot upon the fire to boil. No doubt the oil merchant was really the bandit chief who had brought his men into the yard inside the oil jars. That she guessed. She also realized that she and Ali were to be killed that night.

When the pot of oil was bubbling on her stove, Morgiana filled a saucepan from it and took it quietly into the yard; there she lifted each jar's lid and poured the boiling oil upon the head of every would-be assassin – just enough to scald and kill the man inside. As soon as her job was done, she put out the lamp and waited in the dark to see what would happen next.

At last she heard the chief of the thieves get up, open the window of his room and, since all was as silent as the grave, toss down some stones into the yard.

It was the signal.

But to the chief's surprise, no one stirred. He threw more stones and heard the clanging as they bounced off the jars. Still nothing moved. By now he had grown uneasy and, going softly into the yard, lifted the lids of every jar and found his gang of bandits dead – all scalded by the boiling oil. In his fright he scrambled over the courtyard wall and took to his heels, not stopping until he had reached the cave.

Morgiana poured in the boiling oil.

This time he would not fail!

When Morgiana saw his hasty departure, she went gratefully to bed, thanking Allah for their lucky escape. Only in the morning did she tell Ali Baba of the plot and show him the gruesome contents of the jars.

'O my beloved wife,' Ali cried, 'I owe my life to you and will remember your brave deed for the rest of my days.'

Throughout the day Ali was busy digging holes in his garden in which to bury the bodies of the thieves. Meanwhile, his wife went off to market to sell the nineteen mules. No one in the city must be any the wiser about the night's events.

Not far from the city, meanwhile, the robber chief was sitting in his cave, plotting revenge upon Ali and Morgiana. This time he would not fail, that he pledged upon the memories of his band of thieves. But first he had to don a new disguise: cutting off his black whiskers and fixing on a long grey beard, he dressed himself in the finest silks from his cave.

'I shall call myself Cogia Hussein,' he said, looking at himself in a mirror. 'And I'll find a way of penetrating Ali Baba's house.'

Returning to the city, he took lodgings at an inn and, pretending to be a pious merchant, he soon made friends with other merchants in the town. In the passing of the days, this Cogia Hussein met Ali Baba, whom he treated more than once to a sumptuous supper at the inn. Ali wished to return the man's kind hospitality and invited him home to dine – the following Friday being the appointed day.

97

That was the robber's chance: he planned to kill Ali and his wife after the meal.

At the appointed time, the venerable merchant Cogia Hussein arrived at Ali Baba's house. Both Ali and his wife were most impressed by his smooth-tongued courtesy; yet there was something about him that the sharp-eyed woman found amiss. She watched him carefully from beneath her veil as she served the meal, before retiring to another room (as was the custom when men ate together in Persia). Morgiana had noticed something familiar about the merchant's face – despite the silvery flowing beard. She had also spotted the hilt of a dagger outlined beneath his robe – certainly not the sign of a pious guest!

Then she realized: of course, it was the robber chief.

Without saying a word to her husband, Morgiana entered the room to clear away the empty dishes. That done, she proposed that she might dance before her husband and his guest. Ali readily agreed: it would be an honour for the noble merchant. Morgiana whirled about the floor, gliding and leaping, turning so fast she made the golden bracelets on her ankles tinkle like little bells. The robber chief, though displeased at this diversion from his plans, did not object to the entertainment, and was for a moment off his guard.

That was the moment for Morgiana to act: as she whirled past, she suddenly turned, bent down and, in one swift movement, plunged a dagger into his heart.

In horror, Ali Baba cried out, 'Wife, what have you done? Are you mad?'

'It was to save you,' she said, holding the blood-stained dagger above the guest. 'See here . . .'

With that she tore off the villain's beard and pulled the dagger out from his robes. There before them were the cruel features of the chief of the forty thieves.

Yet again Morgiana had rescued her husband from the jaws of death. And to avoid the suspicion of their neighbours, they buried his body in the garden alongside his men. And no one discovered their rotting bones for many, many years, by which time none had concern for the people of this story.

It was a whole year before Ali visited the cave again; and this time he took along his wife to show her what lay within. The overgrown path leading to the rock was proof enough that the cave was undisturbed. With trembling lips, Ali pronounced the password: 'Open sesame.'

And right away the rock swung open to reveal the treasure cave. Morgiana was delighted with the sacks of glittering coin and gems, but she counselled caution.

'Let us take but a modest bag of gold each time we come,' she advised. 'Just enough for us to live in comfort. That way we shall leave plenty for our children's children.'

She turned so fast that she made the golden bracelets on her ankles tinkle like little bells.

Ali Baba and Morgiana lived long lives and, before they died, passed on the secret of the cave to their children; and they in turn handed it down, so that to this very day the descendants of Ali Baba still use the cave somewhere in Persia to make them rich.

The Merchant and the Genie

ONCE UPON A TIME there was a wealthy merchant who traded far and wide. One time he set off by camel to foreign parts, taking with him a saddle bag of biscuits and dates as provisions. As he journeyed across a desert, he stopped at an oasis and sat beneath a tree to take refreshment. After sipping water and eating a date, he tossed away the date stone and thought no more about it.

All of a sudden, however, he saw an enormous genie, sword in hand, bearing down on him.

'Rise, that I may slay you as you have slain my son,' the genie roared.

Amazed as much as he was scared, the merchant asked, 'How then have I killed your son?'

'When you threw away the date stone,' the genie said, 'it struck my son, who was invisible, killing him outright.'

'If I killed him, I did not do so intentionally,' cried the poor merchant. 'Pray pardon me my crime.'

But the genie pushed the merchant to the ground and raised his arm to strike him with the mighty sword. On seeing his end was near, the merchant pleaded desperately, 'Know, O genie, that I have debts to pay, pledges to fulfil. I also have children and a wife to say goodbye to. Let me therefore go back home and settle my affairs, then I'll return to you to take my punishment. As Allah is my witness, I vow to return so you can do with me as you will.'

The genie stayed his hand awhile, thinking. At last he spoke: 'Go then, but be back within a year.'

So the merchant returned home, accomplished all he wished, paid what he owed and informed his family of his misadventure. When the year was up, he donned his funeral clothes, bade a tearful farewell to his wife and children and went forth the way he had come.

Eventually he came to the tree where he had rested a year before. And as he sat there, weeping for his coming death, an old man came up leading a gazelle upon a chain. The man greeted the merchant, wished him long life and enquired why he was sitting alone in that eerie place – since an evil genie lived thereabouts.

The genie raised his arm to strike the merchant with the mighty sword.

They saw a huge twirling
pillar of smoke fast
approaching from the desert.

The merchant gladly told his tale, at which the man exclaimed, 'By Allah, brother, you are a faithful man. I shall remain beside you and see what will come to pass.'

As the owner of the gazelle was waiting with the merchant, a second man approached, this one leading two black hounds. He also wished to know why they were sitting in such a fearful place. And he too was told the story from start to end. Thereupon he also decided to remain.

Soon after, in the distance, they saw a huge twirling pillar of smoke fast approaching from the desert. As it came closer, the smoke slowly faded and there stood the genie, sword in hand, his eyes shooting sparks of fire. He bore down upon the three men and dragged out the merchant, crying, 'Rise, that I may slay you as you slew my son!'

The merchant and the two men with him began to wail and weep. And then the owner of the gazelle threw himself at the genie's feet, kissed one of his toes and said, 'O genie, crown of the genie kings, I wish to tell you the wonderful story of myself and this gazelle. If it pleases you, will you grant me half of your claim to the merchant's life? Please, I beg of you.'

For a while the genie thought, and then, since he enjoyed good stories, gave his consent.

'If you relate to me a story that is as wonderful as you say, I will give up half my claim to the merchant's life.'

'Then harken to my tale, O genie,' said the man, and proceeded to tell his story.

'This gazelle is really my uncle's daughter, part of my own flesh and blood. I took her as my wife when she was but a girl, and lived with her some thirty years; but Allah did not bless us with a child. So I took a slave girl and soon had a son as handsome as the rising moon. My son grew up in peace and happiness. However, one day, when he attained the age of fifteen years, I had to make a journey to a distant town to try and sell some of my wares.

'Now, unknown to me, my first wife was a sorceress, and while I was away she changed my son into a calf and his mother into a cow. Thus, when I returned and asked after my son and his mother, I was told the slave-girl was dead and my son had disappeared. On hearing this I mourned deeply for a whole year until the festival of sacrifice, when I told my herdsman to choose a cow for me to slay. He brought me one, but in truth it was the slave-girl whom my wife had bewitched. I took a knife and prepared to slit the cow's throat. The animal moaned and cried piteously; all the same, I killed and skinned it. To my surprise, however, inside its skin I found naught but bones no bigger than those of a young girl. Thereupon, I instructed my herdsman to fetch me a fatted calf.

'And he brought my son.

'As soon as the calf saw me it broke its rope and ran towards me,

103

crying so piteously that my heart was moved to spare it. Despite my wife's insistence that I slaughter it, I sent the calf back to the herd unharmed.

'Next day, my herdsman came up in great excitement, saying he had some amazing news: his daughter, who had learned magic from a wise woman, had recognized the calf as my long-lost son. He and his mother, whom I had already slain, had been enchanted by my wife.

'I laughed and cried in turn, overwhelmed with relief that he was not dead and grief for his mother slaughtered by my hand. I bade the herdsman bring forth his daughter and the calf; and there before my eyes the girl sprinkled the calf with water and – Allah be praised – it turned three somersaults and became my son again. How overjoyed we were: we hugged and kissed and cried together.

'But that was not all. At my request, the maiden wove a spell upon my wife to stop her evil ways. And she was turned into the gazelle you see before you.

'That is my story, oh genie.'

'It is indeed a wondrous tale,' the genie said. 'I readily concede to you half my claim to the merchant's life. And much good will it do you!'

At that, the second man, owner of the two black hounds, came forward and threw himself at the genie's feet, crying, 'If I relate my story and you find it likewise amazing, will you grant me also half your claim to the merchant's life?'

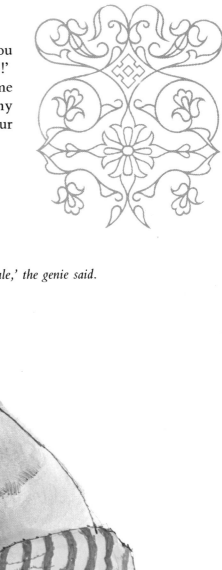

'It is indeed a wondrous tale,' the genie said.

Since he could not resist another story, the genie grudgingly consented, though he badly wanted to kill the man.

'Then,' said the second man, 'know, O lord of genies, that these two hounds are, in truth, my brothers. Our father died and left us three thousand pieces of gold to share between us. With my thousand I opened a shop to buy and sell prayer mats and carpets. I worked hard and prospered, while my two brothers travelled widely and lost all they had. On their return, they tried to persuade me to travel with them, saying I would bring them luck. It was six years before I consented, then I prudently buried half my fortune of six thousand pieces of gold and shared out the rest – a thousand pieces each. With that we bought some merchandise, hired a sailing ship and set sail to make our fortune. Within a month we arrived at a port where we sold our wares, receiving ten pieces of gold for every one we spent.

'But just as we were about to set sail for home, a ragged maiden approached me on the shore, kissed my feet and begged me to take her with me, promising to repay my charity with love and devotion.

'When I looked at her, my heart was moved with tenderness and pity. I took her with me, clothed her richly, gave her a place of honour on board the ship and treated her with kindness and respect.

'But in the company of this sweet maiden, I neglected my brothers and they, in consequence, grew jealous of me, my companion and my wealth. Jealousy is a sinful sickness that poisons mind and heart. And as soon as we had put to sea, my brothers crept up on the maiden and me while we slept, and tossed us into the depths.

'Yet as soon as the girl touched the water, she turned into a genie: straightaway, she lifted me up and soared with me through the air until we reached the courtyard of my house. After putting me safely down, she disappeared.

'I went straight to my hiding-place, dug up the three thousand pieces of gold and opened up my shop again. I prospered as before, but one day was surprised to have a visit from the captain of my old ship, leading two black hounds. He told me a strange tale – that my brothers had mysteriously vanished on board, yet two strange dogs had been found barking in their cabins. Like the captain, I had no idea who the two hounds were nor where they had come from. But on seeing me they whined and licked my hand; their eyes seemed to want to tell me something.

'At that moment, the genie who had saved my life appeared, telling me that the dogs were, in truth, my own brothers. She had turned them into hounds as punishment; they would remain as such for ten long years before they could take their proper shape again.

'That was ten years ago to this very day; I am on my way now to that genie so that she can restore them. That is my story.'

When the second man had finished, the genie shook with delight, for

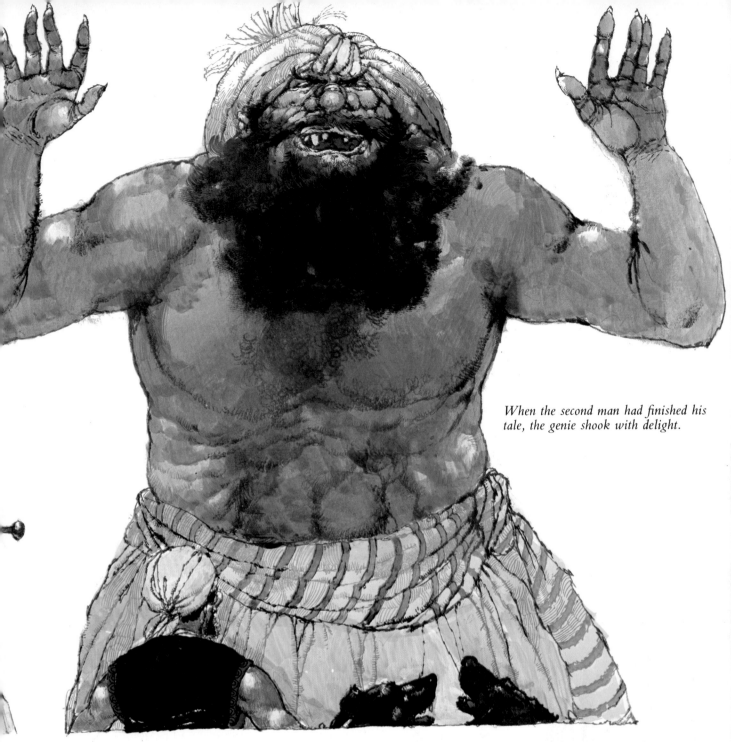

When the second man had finished his tale, the genie shook with delight.

not only did he enjoy the story, he also knew the female genie who had saved the man. He therefore gave up his claim to the merchant's life.

Then with a roar and swirl of dust, he whirled round and round, disappearing across the desert in a great corkscrew of smoke. The merchant, of course, did not fail to thank his two friends whose tales had saved his life. Bidding farewell, each man proceeded on his way: one with the gazelle, one with the two black hounds, and one in his funeral attire.

And thankfully the merchant returned home to his delighted wife and children, passing the rest of his days in peace.

107

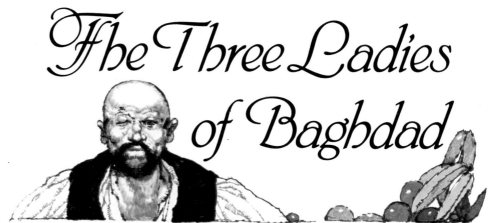

The Three Ladies of Baghdad

IN THE TIME OF THE GREAT CALIPH OF BAGHDAD, Haroon Al-Rashid, there was in the city a one-eyed porter with a shaven head, a man of wit and wisdom. One day, as he was sitting in the bazaar waiting for work, a veiled lady approached; when she raised her gold-embroidered veil to speak he caught a glimpse of her beautiful face.

'Bring your baskets and follow me,' she said.

Willingly the porter followed in her wake as she went about the market buying wares. First she stopped at the fruiterer, purchasing two jars of wine, Syrian apples and Oman peaches, jasmin from Aleppo, water lilies from Damascus and cucumbers from the Nile.

'Put them in your baskets,' she instructed the porter.

They were followed by Egyptian limes and Sultanee lemons, olives and sweet-scented myrtle, sprigs of the henna tree, chamomile, anemones and violets.

'Put them in your baskets,' she said.

Next, she bought ten pounds of meat wrapped in a banana leaf, dried fruits and a dish of Turkish Delight. All of it went into the porter's baskets, which were now heavy. 'If you had told me how much you were going to buy, I would have brought my mule,' he said with a wry smile upon his face.

The lady smiled too, but continued her purchases at a perfumerers: rosewater, musk, frankincense, aloes-wood, ambergris, orange water and, finally, wax candles.

'Take up your baskets and follow me,' she said.

The poor porter staggered along behind her, one basket upon his back, until they came to a splendid mansion. Gently the lady knocked upon the door, and it was opened by a tall, graceful woman with eyes as lovely as a gazelle's, eyebrows like the new moon at Ramadan and cheeks like anemones. When the porter saw her he stood as if in a trance.

'Do come in,' the first lady said to him. 'Bring the baskets into the kitchen.'

And she led him through a large green courtyard, past spouting fountains, and into a richly-furnished room. At the far end stood a red satin couch on which was seated a third woman – the most beautiful of all. As the porter stood in the centre of the room, lost for words amidst such beauty, the lady rose from the couch and came towards him.

'My cousins,' she said, 'do you not see this honest man is about to drop from his burden? Let us ease him of it.'

Together they lifted down the baskets, unpacked the provisions and gave the porter two pieces of gold. Instead of leaving at once, he seemed glued to the spot: for he had rarely seen such beauty and splendour before. Thinking that perhaps the reward was not enough, the third lady said, 'Give him another piece of gold.'

At that the porter found his tongue: 'By Allah, mistress, my hire is but two nusfs; you have paid me too much already. Forgive my rudeness: my heart and mind were taken with my thoughts of you – three ladies all alone with no man to amuse you with his company. A minaret, after all, stands firmly on four walls and not on three. Likewise, the pleasure of women is not complete without the wit of men.'

'We need no man to amuse us,' the first lady replied. 'Men would not keep our secrets, for as the poet says:

> Guard thy secret from a man;
> Entrust it not to him.
> For she who tells a man a secret
> Will lose it forever.

'But I am trustworthy,' replied the porter. 'And I would say to you: only a faithful person keeps a secret. A secret with me is as in a locked house whose key is lost and whose doors are sealed.'

Though he had but one eye and looked odd with his shaven head, the women were attracted by the fellow's wit.

'You presume too much,' the first lady said. 'But if my cousins agree, you may stay with us awhile and entertain us. First let me introduce us: I am Amina, the second lady you met is Safia, and the third is Zubaida.'

'Yes, let him remain,' Safia said, 'but on one condition: you must keep our secrets and ask no reason for anything you see. After all, he who speaks of things that do not concern him shall hear things that will not please him.'

Zubaida meanwhile prepared a table by the fountain in the courtyard and set it with wine and sweetmeats. The porter sat down as if in a dream with the three ladies, drinking and feasting with them until all were merry and at ease. Then, as the evening drew on, Amina suddenly arose, saying to her cousins with a sigh, 'Come, clear the table. I must do my duty.'

With that, she walked across the yard and soon returned leading two black dogs on chains. Handing them to Safia, Amina tucked up her sleeves, took down a whip from the wall, and said gravely, 'I am ready, bring one here.'

At once the dog began to whine and howl, cowering from the whip. Paying no attention, Amina fell to whipping it without mercy until her arms were tired. She must have given it at least a hundred lashes. To the porter's surprise, she then pressed the dog to her bosom, kissed its head and wiped away its tears with her own hair.

'Now bring the second,' she said, giving the first dog to her cousin.

And the same cruel procedure was followed as before. When the beatings were done, all three ladies were in tears and the dogs were led out limping and whimpering from the yard.

So distraught was Safia that she fell to the ground in a swoon; her companions, running to her, loosened the neck of her dress to give her air. The porter was surprised and not a little horrified to see cruel scars and weals upon her fair smooth skin.

111

Up till now he had kept his peace; but he could contain himself no longer. Forgetting the promise he had made to ask no reason for what he witnessed, he exclaimed, 'Mistresses, tell me the meaning of these strange events: the two black dogs and your cousin's scars.'

As his voice broke through their sobs, the ladies rose, facing him sternly.

'How dare you speak,' Safia said. 'You promised to hold your tongue. Is it not enough for us to admit you to our house and feed you well? Now you must be punished!'

With that she stamped her foot, shouting out, 'Slave, come here at once!'

Immediately, a door opened and in came a huge slave, a sharp curved scimitar in his hand.

'Shall I strike off his head, mistress?' asked the slave.

The poor porter, certain his end was near, pleaded with the ladies, 'Do not kill me, I beg of you. Let me tell you the story of how I lost my eye and dark brown hair. And then, should my story not amuse you, by all means strike off my head.'

The ladies whispered among themselves and finally agreed. So the porter began his tale.

The Porter's Tale

My father was a King whose brother ruled a neighbouring land to ours. I was born on the same day as my uncle's son and, as we both grew up, we took turns each year to visit one another. When I was fifteen, I paid my customary visit and after we had dined well and drunk much wine, my cousin asked for a favour. Readily I agreed, though I knew not what the favour was.

Thereupon my cousin went off, returning shortly afterwards with a beautiful young girl, about the same age as ourselves. He bade me follow him as he and the girl set off through the town, until I found myself amid the graves and tombs of a cemetery on the outskirts. Coming to a tomb, my cousin unlocked the stone door and descended some steps into a room; in the corner stood a shovel and a bowl of wet cement.

As I looked on dumbly, still affected by the wine, my cousin picked up the shovel and dug away some earth from the centre of the room, until he had uncovered a flat stone; raising that, he revealed a winding staircase down which he and the girl immediately climbed. Turning back, he asked me to replace the flat stone and the earth, and to use the cement to seal the tomb's entrance. Thereupon he bade farewell and descended the steps.

In my stupor I did exactly as he instructed before returning to my uncle's palace; and there I went to bed. I slept soundly until late

My cousin bade farewell and descended the steps.

*The one-eyed Vizier stood
before me with revenge
upon his face.*

morning, waking up abruptly as from a dreadful dream. Only then did I repent of what I had done.

In haste I returned to the graveyard and searched amongst the tombs, but – oh horror! – I could not find the tomb of the night before. I searched and searched all day until night drew its dark veil about me and I could see no more. Back to the palace I went in great despair. Luckily, my uncle was away hunting and would not return for seven days, so in my remorse I left for home before his return. I could not face his rage and grief.

But more misfortune was to follow. No sooner had I reached my father's capital than guards fell upon me, informing me that the King was dead and his Vizier had seized power.

Now, the Vizier and I were old enemies, for as a boy I had once shot an arrow at a bird, missed and put out the Vizier's eye. I had been beside myself with grief and shame, but my tears had not appeased him. At that moment the one-eyed Vizier stood before me with revenge upon his

114

face. Suddenly, before I could move, the evil man thrust his finger in my left eye and pulled it out.

So, dear ladies, I became as you see me now.

The Vizier then had me taken from the city and cast out on the plain, to be devoured by wild beasts. Fortune, however, was kind and I made my way unharmed to my uncle's land. Though I told him of my father's fate, I kept silent about his son – in spite of his grief at the prince's disappearance. However, as the days went by and my uncle's tear-stained face began to haunt my dreams, I had to confess the truth.

At once my uncle bade me take him to the graveyard; and to my surprise, I found the tomb quite easily. With our bare hands we quickly broke open the sealed tomb door, removed the earth and paving stone, and descended fifty steps. Smoke blinded our eyes and an acrid smell abused our nostrils; but we plunged on through the haze and came upon a charred, smouldering couch. The sight was horrible: upon it lay two young people, now burned to cinders.

My uncle seemed to lose all reason: he spat upon the remains of the bodies and beat their charred and brittle bones with a stick, breaking them into pieces. Horrified at his actions, I tried to restrain him from his wild assault. When at last I had led him from the dreadful tomb, he told me the reason for what he had done.

'O son of my late brother,' he exclaimed, 'those were the remains of my son and the daughter of my worst enemy. When they were very young they always played together, and there grew up a strong love between them. They met secretly as they grew older, knowing I would disapprove of their love and forbid them to see each other. So finally, as you see, since they could not live together upon the earth, they died in each other's arms.'

He suddenly broke down in tears, and I wept with him.

Then he said, 'Henceforth, you shall be my son.'

We stood in silence for a while, me reflecting upon the vagaries of fortune: the sad destiny of the young lovers, my father's murder and the loss of my eye. And I wept again.

But yet more misfortune was to come.

For as we reached the palace gates we heard a great commotion and discovered that my father's Vizier had now captured this city, too.

Grief overwhelmed my uncle: he snatched up a sword and thrust it into his heart, killing himself immediately. As for me, I shaved off my hair (which never grew again) before making my escape, disguised as a holy man. That was seven years ago. I came to the abode of peace and worked as a porter, keeping my secret until this day.

The porter ended his tale and there was silence as the three ladies looked one to the other. After several minutes Amina spoke: 'We pardon you.'

And she dismissed the slave. Then, pouring them all a glass of wine,

she addressed the porter once again: 'Since you have shared your secret with us, we will each tell you our stories. They are even more terrible than your own.'

First to begin was Amina.

Amina's Tale

The two black dogs are, in truth, my sisters. I am the youngest of the three. After my father died, leaving five thousand pieces of gold, my two sisters married and gave their husbands as dowry a thousand gold coins each. With this money they purchased merchandise and set off on a journey to build an even bigger fortune.

Four years went by.

The husbands lost all their money, abandoning my sisters in a foreign land. The poor women returned to me as beggars, and I hardly recognized them. Yet willingly I took them in and shared my wealth equally. For while they had been away I had used my inheritance wisely and Allah had blessed me with success.

For a year thereafter all went well, then one day I decided to try trading in foreign parts. So I stocked a large ship with silks and spices, inviting my sisters to join me. They readily agreed.

Before setting sail, I divided my remaining money into equal portions: one I took with me, the other I buried beneath my house.

The voyage went well until a sudden squall blew us off course and, after two days of drifting in the storm, we came in sight of an uncharted land. Since we needed fresh water and provisions, we all disembarked and, while the sailors went about their work, my sisters and I wandered into the city to explore. Imagine our surprise when we entered the silent town and found its residents turned to black stone!

Strangely, all else was left unharmed, so as we made our way through the streets and market square we saw stone merchants, dogs and donkeys standing like statues beside silks and wooden carvings, pots and jewellery, rotting fruit and vegetables. While my sisters filled their bags with silks and gems, I proceeded alone towards the palace, walked through its open gates and into the marble entrance hall. There I saw urns of gold and silver, and some half-filled with wine.

In the central hall the Shah himself sat stiff and straight upon his throne amongst his viceroys and viziers, all dressed in silken robes trimmed with gold. Behind the pearl-studded golden throne stood fifty memlook guards holding rusting swords.

I wandered on through the palace halls until I came to the harem, all hung with velvet curtains. The women there were clad in rich coloured gowns, each adorned with strings of pearls, diamond-studded rings and bracelets, still gleaming on black marble flesh.

At the far end of the harem I passed through a door into a small room sparsely furnished with a curtained couch. Something about the room aroused my curiosity: then I realized – there were lighted candles round the walls. They could only have been lit recently, and by none other than a human hand!

Although I searched all the rooms and corridors, upstairs and down, I found no one; it was getting dark by now and I hurried to retrace my steps out of the palace. However, to my consternation, I could not find the door; so in the end I lay down on that curtained couch in the little room. And I fell into a restless sleep.

About midnight I was awakened by a soft, melodious voice reciting verses from the Koran. I rose at once, followed the sound and came upon a young man in a vaulted chapel kneeling on a prayer mat. I asked how he had avoided the fate of his townsfolk. He was surprised and overjoyed to see me, and gladly unburdened his soul.

He explained that he was the son of the Shah whom I had seen seated on the throne. The Shah and all his subjects had been Magians who did not worship God – they swore by light and shade, fire and water, and the life-giving sun within the sky. However, there was one old slave who followed the true faith – Islam. She did so secretly, teaching it to the Prince so that he grew up by the laws of El-Islam, knowing the proper ways to wash and purify himself, to pray and to commit to memory the whole of the Koran.

Amina fell into a restless sleep.

When she died, the Prince was the only Muslim in the city, though no one knew of it. Soon after, a crier walked through the town proclaiming death to all unless they worshipped Allah. He vanished just as mysteriously as he had come. Of course, the Shah calmed his subjects' fears, telling the people to ignore the warning.

But the crier returned. He came a second year and then a third, announcing his warning in a voice of doom. Yet still folk persisted in their ways until one morning the catastrophe occurred. The heavens rumbled, lightning flashed and every living being – man and woman, child and beast – was turned to stone. All except the Prince.

Since then he had spent his days in constant prayer.

The young man, being weary of his lonely state, willingly accepted my proposal to come to Baghdad, the holy city of his faith. His tale had been so long it was now dawn, and we set off together from the palace, taking with us many precious gems. I soon found my sisters with a party of sailors looking for me, anxious for my safety. They questioned me eagerly, and I told them of all I had seen and heard. But instead of rejoicing with me at the young man's rescue, my sisters grew jealous of the Prince and myself, and plotted against us.

We embarked once more and set sail for home. I was exceedingly happy for, truth to tell, I had fallen in love with the handsome Prince and he with me. I dreamed of how we would live in wealth and happiness once home in Baghdad. But I did not count on my sisters' treachery: one night, while the young man and I both slept, my sisters took us up from our beds and threw us into the sea.

My beloved Prince, being unable to swim, was drowned. But I – thanks be to Allah – awoke in time and snatched at a floating log which bore me to land.

All through the night I wandered across the island until at dawn I spotted a neck of land leading to the mainland. Since the sun had risen, I dried my clothes then continued along the path until I was drawing near a shore upon which stood a big city.

Suddenly, I noticed a rabbit hopping across the path followed closely by a large snake; the poor animal was exhausted and was about to be swallowed by the snake. I grabbed a stone, threw it and killed the snake instantly.

I was now so tired that I lay down to sleep beneath a bush; suddenly I awoke to find a young maiden seated at my feet, gently rubbing them with her hands.

'Who are you?' I asked, amazed.

She said she was a genie who had taken the form of the rabbit I had seen. And since I had saved her life, she had already repaid the debt. Whatever could she mean?

'I know your story,' she said, 'and I know of your sisters' treachery. So while you slept I flew to your ship and transported all its riches to your house. As for your evil sisters, I have changed them into dogs; and since they repaid your charity with murder – for I cannot bring the young man back to life – they must suffer eternal punishment: every day you must give them a hundred lashes each. If you do not, beware: I shall turn you into a black dog, too.'

With that, she carried me to my home and all was as she said. Now, therefore, I whip these dogs each day, though it breaks my heart.

All was silent for a while. Then Amina turned to Safia, asking her to tell the story of the scars upon her neck. With a deep sigh, Safia began her tale.

Safia's Tale

At his death my father left me a fortune and I soon married one of the wealthiest men of the age; but sadly my husband died within a year. However, this increased my fortune by eighty thousand pieces of gold, so I lived in comfort and style.

One day, as I was sitting in my splendid home, an old woman entered. She kissed my feet and implored me to attend the wedding of her only daughter; the girl was broken-hearted at having no one of good family to give her away. Since I had devoted my life to charity after my husband's death, I gladly consented and followed the old woman through the town. We finally arrived at a door which opened into a room lit by lamps and candles. The lovely young bride was seated upon a couch, though there was no sign of the groom.

All of a sudden, the old woman threw herself at my feet, confessing the real reason for the invitation. It seems her son had seen me at some festivity and fallen deeply in love; it was he who wished to marry me.

Being curious and, I must confess, a mite flattered too, though I naturally displayed anger at the deceit, I said, 'I take no interest in other men; I respect the memory of my dead husband. But where is this man, that I might tell him to his face?'

At that, the old woman clapped her hands and in came a young man so handsome that my heart went out to him despite myself. We sat and talked, and somehow my tongue could not form the words to dismiss and scold him; on the contrary, I found myself succumbing to his sweet words and professions of love. After we had drunk much wine, the Cadee and four witnesses entered and proceeded to perform the marriage ceremony.

When the deed was done and all had departed, my new husband handed me the Koran, saying he wished me to swear that I would always be faithful to him. I saw no reason to refuse, and as soon as I had sworn by Allah, my husband embraced and kissed me, and love for him took possession of my heart.

For several months we lived together in the utmost happiness. Then

'Just let him kiss you lightly over your veil.'

one day I went to the bazaar, accompanied as always by my husband's mother. While we were seated in the shop of a young merchant, the old woman said she knew him well, and praised him constantly. I told her strictly that the young man's virtues were no concern of mine; I desired only material for a dress before I went home.

With that I handed the man the money and went to go. But he refused the coins, saying he would give the material to me free in exchange for a kiss. Straightaway I handed back my purchase and angrily got up to leave. But the old woman pulled me back. 'What harm will it do?' she said. 'No one will know. You would not be unfaithful if you just offered your cheek and let him kiss you lightly over your veil. No one will ever find out.'

In the end, impatient to get home, I shut my eyes, held my veil tightly over my face and waited for the man to take his kiss. But instead of kissing me, he gave me a savage bite; it was so painful that I fainted on the spot.

When I recovered the shop was closed, the man had gone and the old woman was tending to my wound. She patched it up as best she could,

120

though there was blood still on my veil and gown, not to mention the cruel gash upon my face. We hurried home and I went straight to my room, instructing the servant to tell my husband I was ill.

He came to see me right away, most agitated and concerned about my health. Naturally he saw the wound upon my cheek and demanded in a rage to know its cause.

'I was walking down the street,' I said, 'when a camel loaded with firewood knocked into me, tearing my cheek as it passed.'

At that, my husband threatened furiously to complain to the governor and have every camel-owner in the city put to death. So I had to tell another story.

'No, it was not a camel,' I muttered. 'It was an ass that took fright, knocked me over and cut my cheek with its hoof.'

Thereupon my husband was even more incensed, and threatened to have the governor hang every ass-driver in the city. In desperation, I made up story after story. But it did no good, for the old woman had already told him the truth. Suddenly, my husband seized me violently, dragged me from the bed and threw me roughly to the floor. At his command, the door burst open and in came seven slaves who held me down while he stood, sword drawn above my head.

'I'll cut her in two,' my husband cried, 'and feed the pieces to the fish that swim in the River Tigris.'

I shut my eyes, committing myself to Allah. But suddenly the old woman hobbled in and threw herself across my body, her arms outstretched so that the blade could not touch me.

121

'O my son,' she implored him, 'spare this poor woman for Allah's sake. She has sinned, it is true, but try to find it in your heart to forgive her, just as Allah is all-merciful.'

She wept and kissed his feet, begging for my life until, at length, he put aside his sword.

'Though I spare her life,' he shouted, 'she must forever bear the marks of her disgrace.'

So saying, he ordered the slaves to fetch thorny branches of the quince tree; with these he beat me mercilessly upon the back and front and sides until I fainted from the pain and loss of blood. I was certain I would die.

When the beating was at an end, he ordered the slaves to take me to my former house and leave me there until I recovered. And there I lay for four months till I was well enough to return to my husband's home, head bent in shame. Yet, to my astonishment, the house was gone and the entire street pulled down. Nowhere could I discover the cause, nor the whereabouts of my husband. I was left alone with my scars, and all my fortune gone.

I came to my cousin and told her my story; she, in turn, told hers. So we lived together here until we were joined by our cousin Zubaida, whose story is as sad as it is strange.

Zubaida's Tale, or The Little Hunchback

Unlike my cousins, I married a poor man, a tailor. We loved each other dearly, though we had to struggle to make a living.

One day, while my husband was busy at his work, a little hunchback seated himself in the doorway of our shop; he began to sing and play upon the tabor. So diverting was his music that, at mealtime, we invited him to share our modest fare. But as the little man was eating some fish, a sharp bone stuck in his throat and he choked to death.

This accident greatly alarmed us both, for it might be thought that we had killed the man on purpose.

Now it so happened that a doctor lived close by and we decided to take the hunchback there when it was dark. Thus, late in the evening we carried the body to the doctor's house and knocked at the door. As a servant greeted us, my husband handed her a gold coin, saying, 'Go and tell your master we have a patient for him.'

As the servant mounted the stairs to the doctor's study, we hastily pulled the body up the darkened stairway and left it seated on the topmost step; then we hurried home.

In the meantime, the doctor came quickly to the stairway without turning on the lamp; he stumbled into the body of the hunchback so violently that it fell bumping down the stairs. When the doctor realized what he had done he naturally assumed that it was he who had killed the

fellow. Now he would be punished as a murderer.

In desperation, he and his wife hatched a scheme: they dragged the body up to the roof and let it down their neighbour's chimney. Pulling up the ropes, they made off back to their beds.

Now, this man was a supplier of victuals to the Sultan, providing him with oil, butter, cheese and the like; so he kept a store of such provisions in his house and was constantly bothered by mice and rats. Thus, when he returned home late that night and spotted a figure lurking in his chimney place, he snatched up a poker and rained blows upon him, shouting, 'So it is you, not rats, who have been robbing me!'

The body slumped to the floor and, since it made no protest, the man's anger turned to fear. Pale and trembling, he naturally thought he had beaten the man to death. Now he was for it!

In his terror, the victualler picked up the body of the hunchback, hoisted it on his back and carried it from the house, down the street and to the doorway of a nearby shop; there he propped it by the wall.

Just after midnight, the owner of the shop was returning home from a wedding feast, more than a little merry from the wine he had drunk. Suddenly, as he went to unlock his door, the dead body tumbled upon his back.

Thinking he was being attacked, the merchant knocked his assailant to the ground, hit and kicked him, shouting, 'Thief, robber, help! help!'

His cries alerted the town watchman, who came running up at once. Seeing the shopkeeper laying into the little hunchback, whom he recognized, the watchman stopped the fight and found the little man to be dead. Thereupon the shopkeeper was arrested and taken before the Cadee to account for his crime. A poor hunchback murdered by a shopkeeper was a serious offence!

123

And since the shopkeeper could not deny his crime – after all, he had been caught red-handed – he was sentenced forthwith to death. At once, criers were sent about the town to announce the public execution of the shopkeeper for killing a poor hunchback. The murderer was to be impaled upon a stake.

Just as the execution was about to be carried out, the Sultan's victualler pushed his way through the crowd, confessing that it was he, not the shopkeeper, who was guilty of the crime.

'Let the shopkeeper go,' the Cadee said, 'and put this man to death.'

Thereupon the executioner released the shopkeeper and seized and bound the poor victualler. But just as he was about to drive the sharp stake into this man's body, another figure broke through the crowd. It was the doctor. He confessed that he was the one to blame, explaining how he had done the deed.

So the victualler was released and the doctor seized and bound.

Now, all the while my husband and I had watched this sight in shame. Suddenly, my humble tailor stepped forward and halted the execution; he confessed the real truth of the crime. It was not the shopkeeper, the victualler or the doctor, but he who had caused the little hunchback's death.

And so, with the crowd hushed at this honest scene, my dear husband, the tailor, was put to death. For such is the law: a death for a death.

I was left alone, with no fortune, only shame for my husband's alleged crime; though, since I had prepared the meal, the offence was really mine. Not long after, I left the town and came to live with my two cousins.

There ended Zubaida's tale of the little hunchback. In the silence that followed, she turned to the porter, saying, 'So there we are, three cousins who are the victims of misfortune; that is why we live alone with our secrets.'

The porter was amazed at what he had heard. He felt deep pity for all three women and wondered how he could bring them comfort. Suddenly he had an idea. 'Mistress,' he exclaimed, turning to Amina, 'did not the genie leave you a sign of how she might be called?'

'Yes, she did,' Amina replied, 'though I have never thought of using it. She gave me two tufts of hair and bade me burn them if I wished to summon her; I'll bring them now.'

She left, soon returning with two black tufts of hair. She quickly made a fire, then cast the hair into its midst. Right away the house began to tremble, there was a blinding flash and the genie appeared.

'O genie,' cried the porter, 'I beg of you, undo the spell you put upon these poor souls, for they have surely suffered punishment for long enough.'

The genie smiled, then nodded solemnly; she called for a bowl of water, which Safia at once went to fetch. Uttering some magic words, she sprinkled the water upon the assembled company and the two black dogs. And straightaway the spells that had been cast disappeared: the dogs turned into dark-eyed ladies, their heads bowed low in gratitude; and the scars upon Safia faded away.

Then, as all eyes turned to the porter, the genie sprinkled water on his face. At once his blind eye was restored and thick black hair sprang up upon his head. He became just as handsome as he was once before. In another flash and a puff of smoke, the smiling genie disappeared.

How the happy company rejoiced and hugged one another. Even more food and wine were brought, and rarely can a single man have supped so well amid five such lovely women; this time, it was the thankful porter who served the food.

In the course of time, the porter married Amina, and the other ladies made happy unions with good men about the town.

These stories come to us from the book of tales recorded by the Caliph of Baghdad, Haroon Al-Rashid himself.

Glory be to Allah that they are still told.